Unbreakable Hostage

by

Lauren Shiro

Vanilla Heart Publishing

Unbreakable Hostage

by Lauren Shiro

Copyright 2010 Lauren Shiro

Published by: Vanilla Heart Publishing

www.VanillaHeartBookAndAuthors.com

10121 Evergreen Way, 25-156

Everett, WA 98204 USA

ISBN-13: 978-0615902456   ISBN-10: 0615902456

10 9 8 7 6 5 4 3 2 Second Edition

First Printing, October 2013
Printed in the United States of America

Acknowledgements

To Kimberlee: You put the idea in my head to do a suspense novel. You wanted me to stretch and grow as a writer, and this is what came of that. No matter what I've done, or what I have written, you have fully supported me. You are my teacher, my mentor, my publisher, and my friend. I owe you big time for this one. And maybe this will teach you to plant ideas in my head!

To Chelle: Thank you again for being a good friend; a great writer; a teacher, and a mentor. I have learned and grown so much thanks to you. Thank you for helping me to grow as a writer and a person!

To Jeffrey: Thank you for listening to me ramble about my struggle in trying my hand at something new! You're an incredible suspense writer, and I owe you many thanks for inspiring and encouraging me through this process. Your support, advice & guidance mean more to me than words can ever fully describe!

Chapter 1

Lareina meticulously brushed and blow dried her thick black hair. She watched herself carefully in the mirror as she did so. Lareina always tended to the smallest of details with everything in her life. She also enjoyed looking and dressing well. Tonight was no exception. Tonight, she was going back to school again. She still couldn't believe it was actually happening.

She had been teaching math at a local high school for several years now. She already had her master's degree. She loved math – especially algebra - and she loved the idea of reaching her students, but she didn't feel that she was actually touching their lives as much as she had hoped. Her students hated math. Math meant nothing to them. Lareina couldn't even try to count the number of times her students talked back and told her what a waste of time it was. It seemed that no matter what she did; no matter what new approaches, methods or techniques she used, they still abhorred the boring but necessary subject.

Lareina fought to keep her students interested, but nothing ever worked. Day after day, Lareina felt her spirit was being crushed by the students' severe lack of interest. Lareina wanted more, though; she wanted so much more than this mediocre teaching job was giving her. She wanted to teach students who shared her passion.

So, she decided to make a change. She was going to UCLA to get her Ph. D. in order to teach university level students. The positive environment, and working with students who also loved algebra would be a good change for Lareina. This was absolutely the right decision, she told herself.

Lareina Oliveira was a short Hispanic woman. She and her family had moved to America - to Los Angeles - when she was ten years old; and yet to this day, she still had a noticeable accent.

She stood at only five feet tall. Her skin was a glowing olive color. Her hair was as black as a moonless night sky. She had mesmerizing hazel eyes. Like many Hispanic women, she was quite buxom, but she also had a tiny waist, and great curvy hips. She was nearly perfectly proportionate. With a figure of 34-26-36, she had the ideal hour-glass body.

Throughout her life, Lareina had been approached by numerous men for everything from a fun, friendly night out to one night stands. She even had limitless offers for modeling work, but she turned them all down. Her passion was in mathematics and algebra. Her parents had sacrificed so much for her to have a good life and education here in the United States. She wanted to thank them by pursuing a good education and career. Although she was flattered that so many found her to be beautiful; math was her world, and always would be. She made sure that no one or nothing would ever change that.

She finished brushing her thick, shiny, jet black hair. This was her first day towards her goal of acquiring a Ph. D. Today was her day in working towards a new, rewarding life.

Excitedly, she grabbed her purse and ran down stairs. She left a quick note for her roommate, Sandy, on the kitchen table.

The University of California started classes before the local high schools, so Sandy was enjoying the remainder of her summer vacation while she could.

Lareina and Sandy were an interesting, if not comical, pair. They had met through work: they both taught at the same high school. Working together and living together for several years, the girls had a tight bond. They supported each other; encouraged each other; were always open and honest with each other, and they also liked to tease each other. Lareina was the Hispanic woman who taught math; Sandy was the white woman who taught Spanish. They often joked about the irony of their teaching jobs. Even after several years, they still had a great friendship and were perfect roommates for each other.

Lareina left a short, quick note reminding Sandy that she would be in class, but that she would be home for dinner.

She looked at her license plate as she walked to her truck which was quietly parked in the garage. Her license plate read, "X is 2." It was the closest she could get to having it say, "X equals two." Her license plate was proof that Lareina absolutely adored algebra. Lareina chuckled to herself as she got into her black Chevrolet S-10 king cab truck and drove through the streets of Los Angeles to reach the University in time.

Lareina sat at the front of the classroom. She enjoyed being in the front of the room, right in front of the professor. She felt she would get the most out of the lectures by being front and center. She was also the type that could be distracted, and she did not want to ruin this opportunity. This, the first of many classes, was far too important for Lareina to lose her focus.

As she set her books on her desk, a corpulent man passed by her desk. Like so many men before him, he did a double take when he saw Lareina. He stared, taking in Lareina's stunning looks. Slowly, nearly breaking his neck as he did so, the fat man walked to the back of the classroom while still watching Lareina.

Soon after, the professor walked in. She was a tall, thin, regal woman. Her hair was chocolate brown, pulled back into a tight bun. She wore thick glasses. She looked to be a woman in her mid-sixties or so. Despite her age, though, her features were lovely and surprisingly beautiful.

"This is a Ph. D. level class," the professor started as soon as she walked into the classroom. "I expect a full effort from each and every one of you. If you are in this class, you should be pulling straight A's. I demand a lot of my students, in order to weed out the ones who are not Ph. D. material. Is that clear?" The teacher's voice was cold and strong. "My name is Doctor Bauer. I am here to teach, not to be your best friend. I will, however, work with you if need be.

"Now, let's go through roll call."

"The roll call should be pretty short," Lareina thought to herself. There were very few students in this class. Hopefully, they were all as dedicated as she. Being surrounded in a positive, enthusiastic environment was very important to Lareina. She quietly prayed to that this class would be the constructive setting she so desperately wanted.

"Brian Albertson?"

"Here," a voice from the other side of the room called back.

"Shelly Brighton?"

The girl sitting at the desk next to Lareina said, "Here."

"Anthony Covelli?"

"Here, and please call me Tony." It was the large man who had walked passed Lareina before. He was sitting at the back of the classroom, in the same row as Lareina; almost as if to watch her from behind.

"Gerald Henry?"

"Here!" Another male voice called out.

"Justin Nichols?"

"Present," yet another male voice called out.

"Lareina Oliveira?"

"Here, Doctor Bauer," Lareina said gently since Dr. Bauer was standing right beside her.

Dr. Bauer leaned over Lareina's desk. "Impressive. You are one of only two women in this class. I will expect much from you," the doctor said quietly to Lareina.

"Yes, ma'am," Lareina softly replied.

"And lastly, Phillip Stanley?"

"Here," the last male voice called out.

"Ok, good. You're all brave enough to show up on the first day of class. That's a good sign.

"I've taught many a class where the wimps don't even try on the first day. This means that I expect each and every one of you in class every session in this semester unless there are extenuating circumstances. And by the way, a cold or an upset stomach is not an extenuating circumstance.

"Here's my syllabus for the semester. I highly suggest that you read it thoroughly after we go through it here, so that you fully understand my expectations for this class," Doctor Bauer said as she walked through the fairly empty classroom passing out the thick packet.

Lareina walked to her truck after the four hour class was over. She knew this would be an intense program, but she was prepared. Luckily, since she arrived at the University early, she was able to get a parking spot near to the entrance of the building.

She loaded up her truck with her books and her bag, and then finally pulled herself up and in. She started the truck and drove off.

Tony Covelli sat in his old, tired, red 1984 Mustang and watched Lareina's every movement. She was beautiful. He really wanted to get to know her. He caught a glimpse of her license plate. "X is 2, eh? I'll have to remember that," he whispered to himself.

It took his aged, worn car several tries before it started up. Once the car finally started, he drove off.

Chapter 2

"So, how was class?" Sandy asked at dinner. She had her light brown hair pulled into a ponytail. She must have been at the beach: her typically light skin showed that she had been out enjoying the late summer California sun. Her green eyes twinkled brightly in contrast to her darkening face.

"It was alright. This is definitely going to be a heavy workload, but I knew that going in. It's a small group of students, but that's ok. I'm guessing that they are all as determined as I am, so I think that overall it's going to be a good situation for me.

"How about you? Do you have all your lesson plans and everything laid out for the new school year yet?"

"Yeah. But I just got a call from Rob Dunn while you were in class. Get this: Daniel Gonzales isn't coming back this year for some reason, so now I have to teach his advanced placement class too!"

"Wow! You're kidding?! Boy, I'm really surprised. I wonder why Daniel isn't coming back. He's a good teacher, and he always seemed happy there. I mean, he's been teaching there for ages!"

"I know, it's very weird. I don't know why he's not coming back, Lareina. Whatever the reason is, I'm now stuck with his classes too."

"Do you have to come up with your own lesson plans for that?"

"Thankfully not. There's a protocol we have to follow to prep the students for the actual AP test. It just means that I, too, will have a heavier workload this year.

"You know, I've never taught an AP class before. I just hope that it'll go well."

"You'll be fine," Lareina comforted her friend. "You're the best white girl who speaks Spanish that I know," she teased. "And besides, you're a great teacher too."

"Hello, Mama?"

"Hello, Lareina." Consuelo, Lareina's mother, had a very heavy Hispanic accent, but she wanted the family to speak in English as much as possible. Early on Lareina had been taught that the family had sacrificed greatly to come to this country, so they were to live as true Americans.

"I started classes for my doctorate today."

"Really? How was it?"

"It's going to be a lot of work, Mama. But I know I can do it."

"Oh, I am so proud of you, Lareina. We came from nothing, and you have worked and studied so hard. You took advantage of all that an American education could give you and now look! You will teach the university math."

"I'm doing it for you, Mama. And for Papa, too."

"Thank you, mija. You know how much we love and appreciate you. It is so wonderful for your father and me to see you having opportunities like this: opportunities you'd never have in Puerto Rico."

"Thank you, Mama. Thank you for giving Juanito and I these chances. I don't think either of us could imagine not having such wonderful chances at life. So, thank you."

"You're welcome, mija. You know your father and I would do anything for you two wonderful children.

"So mija, how is Sandy?"

"She's doing well. She'll actually be teaching more classes this year."

"Really? Wow! Good for her!" Lareina's mother paused before saying a familiar joke to Lareina. "Does she still have her American accent?"

Lareina chuckled. "A bit. I still keep trying to teach her real Spanish, but you know how those American girls are."

Consuelo laughed. "You have to teach her to speak it right!"

"I will do my best, Mama.

"Oh, look at the time!" Lareina hadn't realized how late it was when she called her mother. "I should go. I really need study before bed.

"But before I go, are you and Papa ok?"

"Yes, mija. We are both doing well. You are so sweet to always check on us."

"You know I worry about you."

"I know, and your father and I both appreciate it."

"Ok, Mama. I'll call you once I get into a good study schedule routine."

"Alright, my beautiful, smart daughter. I love you."

"I love you too. Tell Papa I love him."

"I will, mija. Adios."

"Adios, Mama."

At the next class session, Tony Covelli, the large man who had ogled Lareina at the last class session, stopped by her desk to try to converse with her. He had become so infatuated with her that he had to try to instigate some kind of communication between them.

"Hi," he said.

He was rather short for a man. He only stood at about five-foot eight. His hefty weight only made him appear shorter. He had thick, dark brown, curly hair. His goatee was thick and bushy as well.

His voice was wretched. Lareina felt uncomfortable and uneasy around him for some unknown reason. His presence made her skin crawl.

Despite her ill ease, she tried to remain polite and pleasant. "Hi," she weakly replied, hoping it would send him away.

"Tough class, huh?"

"Uhhh...no. Not really." Lareina's answer was short and curt. She thought it was odd for a Ph. D. level student to find Dr. Bauer's class difficult.

"Well...ummmm...I mean not for people like us. But for everyone else I'm sure it is," he frantically tried to recover his fallen pick up line.

Lareina looked at her watch. "Class will be starting soon; perhaps you should get to your seat before Dr. Bauer comes in."

"Good idea. Thanks." He smiled at her awkwardly for a few minutes. Eventually, he walked away.

Lareina tried desperately to shake the unusual and icky feeling she got from Tony. It was time to focus on math, not some strange, clumsy man.

Moments later, Dr. Bauer walked into the room and began another intense four hour class.

As class let out, Lareina could feel Tony come up behind her. After grabbing all of her belongings, she looked up at him. Again, that creepy feeling overwhelmed Lareina. Something was not right about this man, she just knew it. "Can I help you, Tony?"

"Oh well, I was just wondering if you'd like me to walk you to your car."

"Oh, well...ummm...thank you, Tony. But I'm fine, really. My parking spot is very close to the building, and it's right under a light so I'll be fine. But...uhhhh...thank you, though."

"Oh, ok." He stepped back and watched her leave the classroom. He waited behind her and watched her walked out to her truck, from a distance.

Lareina shuddered feeling his eyes pierce her straight through to her soul from behind. She silently walked to her truck, desperately trying to shake that unnerving feeling she felt from being around Tony.

Tony sighed as Lareina walked away. He knew he had to come up with better things to say to her, or better ways to get her attention. One way or another, he wanted to be sure they spoke and interacted more. He was far too smitten with this Latin beauty to let her slip through his fat fingers.

Chapter 3

The semester was moving along well, though two people had dropped out of Lareina's class. It was a very challenging program, even harder than Lareina had originally anticipated. It was understandable that not everyone could handle the work load. Losing two students out of an already small class was rather significant, but Lareina and the other students were staying strong in the class. They did not find the class to be too overwhelming. Everyone worked hard, and the class moved at a smooth but quick pace.

Lareina spent every spare moment she had studying. Though she still worked occasionally as a substitute teacher, her free time was fully dedicated to her studies. Her hard work was paying off throughout the entire semester: her strong grades were a good reflection of her efforts.

Sandy was also working hard as she was teaching several classes at the high school. Her schedule was busy and sometimes even hectic, but she handled her work load well.

Despite their full schedules, the two women still shared dinner together almost every night in their home.

One particular evening, the two women shared a typical, nice, light dinner conversation. As usual, it focused around teaching and work: the subjects that the two women seemed to discuss endlessly.

"Bruce Douglass misses you, Lareina," Sandy said.

"Awe, he is such a sweet man. And a great teacher, too! Please tell him I say hello."

"I will.

"You know, he keeps asking when you're coming back. I've told him that you're done with teaching high school students."

"I'm just done teaching L. A. high school students who don't care, Sandy. There's a big difference."

"I know, I know. He just wishes you would stay. He always talks about what a great teacher you are. He's told me on numerous occasions how teachers like you are way too few and far between. He also hates the fact that you went down to just subbing and that he doesn't see you every day any more like he used to."

"That's really sweet. I appreciate his respect for me and my teaching abilities. Coming from him, that means a lot to me."

"Lareina, he even told me that he'd try talking to Dunn, or even the superintendent to try to get you as the head of the department when you're done with school."

"That's very generous of him. But somehow I don't see Dunn, or anyone else for that matter, giving me that job. Dunn likes having men in charge. Come on, you know that."

"I know. He's a sexist principal. I really wish that would change; but for now, it is what it is. But you know, it might not hurt to see if it was actually possible."

"I appreciate the gesture, but I really want to be at a university like UCLA teaching math majors, Sandy. I'd even move if I was offered a position at a place like UC Davis or something."

"You are so stubborn, Lareina."

"I know, but I also have goals Sandy. I can't give up on them now. Think of how disappointed my parents would be."

"Oh I know, Lareina.

"Speaking of them, how are they?"

"They are doing well, as of the last time I spoke to Mama. It's been a little while, but I think they're still doing alright." Lareina paused and took a deep breath. "Hey Sandy? Can I ask you something completely off the subject?" She asked. The tone of the evening suddenly changed drastically.

"Yeah. What's up, girl?"

"Well you see there's this guy in my class named Tony. He kind of creeps me out. I think he's trying to get me to go out with him or something. He constantly hits on me, or walks me to my car – he won't leave me alone! What should I do?"

"Oh the plight of the beautiful!" Sandy teased. "In all seriousness, though, Lareina.Have you just flat out told him 'no'?"

"Yes, of course Sandy! But, then he'll stand near me, or I feel like he's watching me. It's really kind of weird."

"You feel like he's watching you? Oh come on, Lareina! Don't you think maybe you're being too paranoid?"

"No, Sandy, I don't. I don't think I'm being paranoid at all. You don't know – you're not there!"

"Alright, alright. Calm down. Look, if you're that uncomfortable around him, is there anyone else in the class that you can talk to? Hang out with? Have them walk you to the truck?"

"No, none of the other students can help. Not really, anyway. The two other guys in the class have another class right after ours, so they always rush out. And the other girl wouldn't be of any help. She wouldn't deter him. Actually, I don't think anyone or anything would stop him."

"Well, that's too bad. Since that's the case, I don't know what to tell you, Lareina."

"I know," Lareina sighed, and looked at the untouched food that sat on her plate.

The two young women sat in silence for a few moments before Sandy spoke up. "Look, Lareina, the semester is nearly half-way through. Just deal as best you can for the remainder of the session, and then I'm sure you'll be rid of him. It's probably not as bad as you think."

"Yeah, I guess you're right."

As she walked out to her truck after class, Lareina noticed that Tony's beat up Mustang was parked next to her. "Oh great," she said to herself. "He's parked right next to me! I can't ignore him now."

As she began to put her bag and books into the truck, she could hear he was trying to start his car, but it wouldn't turn over. He got out of the dilapidated car, and walked over to her.

"Hey...uhhh...Lareina, do you happen to have any jumper cables?"

Lareina sighed. "Yes. Hang on, let me go get them. While I do that, you need to go open your car's hood."

Lareina opened her back door and then opened her tool set, where her jumper cables were neatly wrapped. She took them out; popped open her hood, and began to hook up the cables to the two cars.

Tony stood back and watched her. He smirked. "Thank you." His tone was grotesque.

"Hang on," she said. She went back to the truck and started it.

Tony began to get into his car to turn it over.

"No, no! Not yet! Let me gas it: it brings more juice to the battery," Lareina called out.

"Oh, ok," Tony said weakly.

Lareina applied pressure to the gas pedal. Her truck slightly roared. She held the gas pedal at that level for a minute, and then let up. "Ok, try it now."

Tony turned over his Mustang, and it started right away.

Lareina jumped out of the truck and began disconnecting the cables from the two vehicles.

Tony ran up to Lareina. "Thanks! Wow, that was really great! I need to thank you for saving the day," he said.

"What? Why? For this? No, no. It's fine, Tony. There's no need to thank me. This wasn't anything special."

"I'd really like to do something to thank you. Would you let me treat you to dinner?"

"Oh!" Lareina exclaimed, startled by his offer. "Ummm...well...thank you for the invitation, Tony. But, I...uhhh...I just don't think it's a good idea. I couldn't. It just wouldn't be right."

"Why? Do you have a boyfriend or something?"

"Well...no. I'm...uhhh...actually not dating right now. I like to focus on my studies – I have a lot of work to do, and ummm...things. So, I try not to be distracted by outside things – or people."

"Oh come on, Lareina! One night out won't hurt."

"Look, I appreciate it, Tony, I really do. But this was nothing, really. I don't think giving your car a jump warrants you taking me out to dinner. You'd spend far too much money for something that cost me nothing.

"Thank you, though."

Tony walked away and quietly sat in his car feeling defeated. He watched infuriated as Lareina walked back to her truck, took her time to put her cables away neatly, and then drove off.

He couldn't believe that she had refused his offer. She had no right to turn him down! Tony hit the steering wheel with his fist. He was so enraged. He wasn't going to let her turn him down again.

"Sandy!"

"What's up, Lareina?" Sandy came down the stairs in a robe and with her hair all wrapped up in a towel.

"He did it again!"

"Who did what when?"

"Remember I told you about that guy, Tony? The creepy one in my class?"

"Oh yeah. So, what happened?"

"Tonight, his car needed a jump. And he was conveniently parked next to me. Me! There are a few other students in class, there are plenty of other cars to park next to, but he specifically picked me!"

"Oh my God! Don't you think that's taking it a bit far, Lareina? I mean come on! Don't you think it might have just been luck or coincidence that he was parked next to you?"

"He asked me out, Sandy! He kept insisting that he take me out to dinner as a way to thank me for jumping his car."

"So?"

"So?! Sandy! Who takes someone out to dinner for jumping their car? I had to turn him down quite a few times! It was like he didn't want to take no for an answer."

"Gees! Look, Lareina, I know he seems creepy to you, but he's probably really harmless.

"Maybe he hasn't dated much. Maybe not many people have shown him that much kindness. Based on what you've said, he's just sounds a bit awkward socially.

"He's probably just uncomfortable being around such a beautiful woman."

"I don't think that's it, Sandy. I really don't. This whole thing is just not sitting right with me."

"Well, did you say yes? Are you going out with him?"

"No! Of course not! I was insistent. I even told him that I don't want to go out or date anyone right now. He knows where I stand with everything."

"Then you'll be fine."

"I don't know, Sandy. It all feels so weird, you know? It's just not sitting right with me."

"Stop being so over dramatic, Lareina. If you're not going out with the guy, you have nothing to worry about."

"I guess you're right. Especially since you seem so sure."

"Yes, I'm sure. It's nothing. You're making a mountain out of a mole hill, I promise."

Another long class session was over, and every one was happy to leave. Lareina packed up and saw that Tony was moving slowly and seeming to stay behind. She took the opportunity to get out to her truck quickly and head back home so she could avoid him all together.

"Doctor Bauer, I need to speak to you," Tony said after everyone had left the classroom. He slowly walked up to Dr. Bauer's desk.

"Yes, Tony. What is it?"

"Well, it's just that I will be out of town on the day of the final exam in order to move my father into a nursing home. I was wondering if I might be able to take the test early."

"Yes, Tony, certainly. I don't see why not.

"Let's see, the final is scheduled for the twelfth."

"May I take it after our final class on the fifth?"

"If you so desire. We'll hold it here in the classroom. Just stay after the lecture, and I will administer the exam to you."

"That would be ideal. Thank you so much for understanding and being so accommodating, Dr. Bauer. I really appreciate it."

"You're welcome Tony," Dr. Bauer said with a sympathetic smile.

Tony walked out of the classroom and smirked to himself. He was quite happy. That had gone very well. He didn't expect Dr. Bauer to be so willing to bend to his needs. This was absolutely perfect for him.

There was only one more month to go in the semester. Things were moving quickly. This last month would be over before he knew it. He could definitely wait one more month.

"Hello, Mama."

"Hola, Lareina."

"How are you and Papa?"

"We are good! Juanito is here tonight. We are all going to have dinner together."

25

"Oh that is so nice! Tell Juanito I say hello and send my love."

"Of course I will.

"How are you, mija?"

"I'm ok, Mama. I have my big final exam coming up in a few weeks."

"Are you nervous?"

"Yeah, a bit."

"Well, do you know the material?"

"Yes, Mama. I study every day, and it all makes sense to me."

"I know you will be fine."

"I hope so."

"How have your grades been so far, Lareina?"

"I've been doing very well. I have a 4.0 GPA average, Mama."

"Oh, that's perfect, Lareina! You have no need to worry, mija. You are very smart. You hold a good average. This test will be simple for you, I am sure."

"That's why I called you, Mama: to feel better. You always know how to reassure me and make me feel better about things."

"I know you will be just fine. You always are."

"Thank you, Mama. I appreciate it.

"I'm sorry; I know I've been talking for a while. I'll let you get back to your dinner with Juanito.

"Adios, Mama. I love you."

"I love you too, mija."

As time continued to tick away and the final exam approached, Dr. Bauer's classes became increasingly more consuming. Lareina focused all of her time and energy on her school work due to the intensity of it all.

Tony Covelli continued to strike up conversations with Lareina at each class session, though. Despite their work load from class, he persisted in asking her out on dates, or trying to include her in other various distractions.

After one particular class, Tony again asked Lareina what her plans were after class.

"Studying, and preparing a lesson plan. I'm teaching tomorrow."

"Oh," he said in a depressed tone. "I was hoping we could get some drinks or something."

"I don't drink, Tony. But, thank you for the offer."

"You don't drink? At all?"

"No, Tony. It's just a choice I made for myself a long time ago."

"Well, you wouldn't have to order an alcoholic drink if you don't want."

Lareina smiled. "Thank you, I appreciate that. Not everyone respects my decision.

"But, I really have to work on that lesson plan so I'm prepared for tomorrow."

"We wouldn't be out late. I promise."

"I'm sure not, but I have not even looked at the curriculum and what I'm supposed to be teaching tomorrow. The worst thing to do is to go into a high school classroom unprepared. I really have to make up a strong lesson plan. I'm really sorry, Tony."

Tony was becoming increasingly aggravated at Lareina's continual dismissals of him. He never let on, however, at just how angry he truly was. Instead, he politely wished her a good evening and left.

Once again, from the safety of his car he watched her drive away. Now that he was alone, he could let his anger consume him. In a matter of moments, his anger turned to determination. Somehow, he was going to make sure that she did not drive out of his life entirely.

One week later, Lareina sat her desk as usual and Tony passed right by her. He didn't stop by to say hello; he didn't even look at her. She thought it was odd that he wouldn't even acknowledge her, especially after his recent advances. She was quite pleased, though. Perhaps he had gotten the hint, or possibly even moved on to a different woman.

Lareina sighed out of relief and waited for another intense session with Dr. Bauer.

After the class, though, Tony walked up behind Lareina as he had done so many times in the past.

"Oh, hi Tony," Lareina said. She was terribly confused by his seeming lack of interest earlier and now his behavior was completely oppositional to that. His behavior didn't seem to make any sense.

"Hey Lareina, some friends and I are getting together tonight to go bowling. I was wondering if you'd like to join us. It wouldn't be a date, just a fun time out with a group of friends."

"Wow, Tony! That is very kind of you. It sounds like it would be a lot of fun, but I simply can't. I promised my roommate that I would help her to prepare an advanced Spanish test for one of her classes; and I have a lot of prepping to do for our final as well.

"I'm really sorry, but please know that I greatly appreciate the offer."

"But all you do is work and study! Don't you think you need a break? Come on! Get some relief and just have fun!"

"It sounds great, it really does. Please don't get me wrong. It's just that I promised my roommate the help, and I can't let her down. Plus, I really want to be sure I'm ready for this final.

"I'm sure you understand that I can't break my promise to her, and that my grades are of the utmost importance. You don't strike me as the type of guy to break a promise. And I know you wouldn't be in this class if you didn't want to do well also. I'm sure you understand where I'm coming from. Thank you, though!"

Lareina got in her car without waiting for a response from Tony. She began to drive away. "So much for him forgetting about me," she said to herself out loud in the car. She pulled away, thinking nothing of the exchange that just occurred.

As she left the university, Tony decided that he needed to see more. He wanted to watch her in her truck. He wanted to see if she was lying to him or not. His Mustang struggled to follow her. He stayed as far behind her as he could, while still being able to keep an eye on her truck. He was able to stay hidden for miles on the Los Angeles freeways.

Tony's body was extraordinarily tense. He gripped the steering wheel tightly; his eyes were narrowly focused on the black truck. He sat forward on the seat, hunched over the steering wheel because of the intensity that was pumping through his veins. He could not understand why her promise to her roommate was more important than his offer.

Though he had no real plans to go bowling, or anyone with whom to go bowling, it didn't matter. He had offered her another night on the town and she refused him. He was going to see what was so much better about home than going out with him.

He continued to drive with an aggravated stare focused solely on her truck.

A few cars moved over unexpectedly and he was suddenly in plain sight of Lareina, despite the distance between them. Out of fear that she might realize it was him, he quickly dashed over and pulled off at the next exit off the freeway.

After coming off the exit ramp, Tony drove to the nearest gas station. He pulled right into a spot and turned off the car. He took a few deep breaths to calm down after the adrenaline rush he just experienced. He couldn't calm down, though. The intense rush was washed over by anger. "You will go out with me," Tony mumbled with fire in his eyes.

Yet another week closer to the final, and once again after class, Tony followed Lareina out to her truck.

29

"Hey Lareina, would you like to grab a bite to eat?" Tony asked the beautiful woman.

"No thank you, Tony. My...uhhh...roommate has already cooked dinner and is waiting for me at home, but I appreciate the offer."

Lareina began to open her car door. Tony quickly grabbed her hand from the car door. His grip was very strong. There was a frightening look in his eyes that Lareina had not seen before. "You always have an excuse. I'm sick of your lies! I don't see why you don't want to spend any time with me. I'm being very generous here. I've given you tons of opportunities for fun and stress relief with me.

"I'm a great guy – you'll never meet another man like me. You'd better stop turning me down. You're being foolish and inconsiderate – that had better stop, and soon!"

Lareina stared at him fiercely. "I will do as I please," she said with great forcefulness. His grasp was firm, but Lareina pulled her arm away, got into her truck and quickly drove away.

"Bitch!" Tony screamed out as her truck sped away.

After one especially excruciatingly long and difficult class, Lareina hurriedly left class, and got into her truck before Tony could approach her. She happily drove home, feeling relieved that she avoided another confrontation with him. His behavior was beginning to concern her greatly. Now that she was safe in her truck, she could relax.

Just a few cars behind her, Tony Covelli followed her home again. He made sure she couldn't see his car this time, but he followed her all over the freeways of Los Angeles. He was tense, angry, frustrated, and determined. He wasn't going to lose her this time. She may have escaped class without speaking to him, but he was not going to let that stop him. He made sure he kept a safe a distance so that she didn't see he had followed her the entire way, even to when she pulled her truck into the garage of her house.

Tony sat in his Mustang, just a few houses down intensely watching her house. He was extremely focused; he refused to let anything distract him from his observation. Neighborhood dogs barked. People walked passed him, but nothing broke his concentration on Lareina's house. "So, this is where she lives," he said to himself. "Not bad."

He sat in his car for hours on end, just watching her house and the silhouettes in the window. The late afternoon slipped into evening, and then night fell, and yet it only felt like a matter of minutes to Tony. Somehow, he just had to have the Latin beauty. The semester was quickly coming to a close. He didn't want to lose out on his chance to be with the amazing woman.

Lareina sat anxiously in her seat. The semester had completely flown by, and now it was time for the final exam. She looked around at the few faces that had stuck with the class during the semester along with her. Oddly enough, Tony was nowhere to be found. Lareina thought that was peculiar, but was she was also relieved by his absence.

After a few moments of nervous silence, Dr. Bauer walked into the room. She immediately dispersed the exams. "This is your final. I expect nothing but perfection from all of you. Otherwise, you don't deserve to continue in this program."

Lareina tentatively opened the first page to the exam, and began her work.

About forty five minutes after beginning her exam, Lareina had finished. She reviewed her work one last time, and then brought the exam up to Dr. Bauer.

"Thank you, Lareina. I look forward to seeing you next semester." Dr. Bauer smiled at one of her best students.

"Yes. Thank you, Dr. Bauer. Have a good holiday vacation."

Lareina was the first to finish the difficult exam, but she felt very confident in her work. She returned to her desk, gathered her belongings, and walked out the door. With her mind reviewing the exam she had just taken, and thinking about her up-coming class with Dr. Bauer next semester, Lareina stepped out into the hallway and walked towards the doors to the parking lot. She didn't look behind her as she heard the door shut to the classroom.

In the hall, she was suddenly grabbed from behind. Lareina gasped from fear. A fat, sweaty hand covered her mouth.

"Don't make a sound," Tony's voice whispered in her ear. His breath was hot and nauseating. "This is a very public place. No one needs to know what's going on. Act naturally, or I'll kill you.

"Walk out with me to my car like everything is normal." Grudgingly, he released her from his grasp. Feeling a sharp object jabbing her in her back, Lareina followed along fearing that Tony might indeed murder her.

They walked out to the old Mustang slowly and carefully. The car was parked far away from the building, in a dim corner. There were no other cars or people anywhere near them. Lareina simply looked straight ahead as she walked, she didn't want to look back at Tony's face.

"Put your stuff in the trunk," he ordered her when they finally arrived at the decaying car.

Still looking forward, Lareina placed her books and bag in the tiny trunk.

"Get in, on the passenger side."

Lareina walked to the passenger door as he directed her; she opened the door and hesitantly sat in the car. Tony got in next to her in the driver's seat.

There was a roll of electrical tape sitting on dashboard. Tony grabbed it and began to unroll it.

"Don't scream or make a move, do you understand me?" Tony leaned down grabbed her ankles and wrapped the tape around them several times. He wrapped them so tightly that the tape was digging into Lareina's skin. Lareina wasn't afraid

32

of Tony; her sole focus was on the newly inflicted pain in her legs.

Tony sat up and grabbed Lareina's wrists. She winced as he touched her. He bound her hands just as tightly as he did her legs.

Tony then pulled the switch on the passenger seat, and Lareina's seat sprung backwards. Lareina fell with a thud.

"Roll completely off the seat and stay on the floor," Tony ordered.

Without saying a word, Lareina undulated and wiggled the rest of her way on to the floor of the back of the car. Tony grabbed her buttocks and helped push her down. The thought of him touching her made Lareina feel sick and dirty.

She lay there and quietly fought to catch her breath. She felt overheated and queasy. Her eyes began to fill with tears. She refused to let Tony see her fear. She lay with her face to the floor so that he would never get the satisfaction of seeing her cry.

"We have a long drive ahead of us. I don't want any problems, and I don't want to have to kill you before we get there, so just do as you're told. Got it?" Tony said.

"Yes," she weakly replied. Lareina closed her eyes and prayed this was all a nightmare.

Lareina wasn't in the house when Sandy came home, or at least that she could see or hear. Sandy thought it was very odd that Lareina would not be home. Wondering if Lareina was sleeping or in the shower, Sandy checked the garage. The truck wasn't even there.

Although it was unusual, Sandy assumed then that Lareina had gone out to celebrate. Or, perhaps she spontaneously decided to spend the weekend with her parents up north, and she forgot to tell Sandy. Whatever the reason for Lareina's absence, Sandy continued on for the remainder of the evening as if everything were normal.

Lareina had been laying in the back of the car for what felt to be an eternity when unexpectedly, the car stopped.

"Yo, Nick!" Tony shouted into his phone over the heavy metal music he had been playing for the entire ride. "You should check out what I got!"

Tony paused for a moment while the person on the other end spoke.

"I'm right here. Look out your window, dummy! Yeah, that's my car! Come on out!"

Lareina could hear a door slam, and then the doors to the Mustang squealed open.

"Look!" Tony said with great excitement.

"Tony, what the hell did you do?" There was another man standing over Lareina, next to Tony. They shared a slight resemblance, but this man's hair was slicked back, and he was clearly older than Tony.

"This is the one I told you about – from class! I got her!"

"You dipshit! As if there ain't enough shit going on with our family," the unrecognizable man said.

"Forget that! That shit doesn't affect me.

"I'm gonna bring her up to the cabin, bro!" Tony's excitement was child-like.

"The cabin?! Are you fucking insane? Everybody knows about that place! Cops will be on you like white on rice! Think, dummy!" The slightly older man hit Tony in the arm.

"It'll be fine, Nick," Tony dismissed the other man's warnings. "Hey...uhh...can I stay for the night? And...uhhh...you got something for her?"

The other man sighed. "Yeah, what are brothers for? Hang on." He then walked away.

"We're stopping for the night, but we still have more driving to do tomorrow, so I don't want to hear a peep out of you," Tony commanded Lareina.

She lay silently on the car floor.

Nick eventually returned with a pill and a glass of water.

"Take this," Tony ordered Lareina. He pulled her so she was sitting upright.

Lareina dared not open her mouth.

With great force, both men grabbed her face and jaw. They pried open her mouth, shoved the pill down her throat and poured the water down her mouth as well. Lareina gagged and choked for a few seconds.

Tony shoved her back down. "You'll be fine here for the night." Tony slammed the car doors shut and began to walk away. Lareina could hear the other man yell at Tony again as they walked away.

Gradually, things became blurry and fuzzy. Though the car wasn't moving, Lareina felt as though she was rocking on a boat in the sea. The world around her swirled and slowed down. Lareina fought the drowsiness as best she could, but it ultimately won. Blackness swept over Lareina and she slept in the back of the car, unseen and unheard.

Chapter 4

The next morning had arrived and there were still no signs of Lareina: no any phone calls; no text messages. Her truck was still missing. Something was terribly wrong. Sandy began to feel ill with worry. What if something had happened to her friend? Not wanting to panic and over react, Sandy first called Lareina's family.

"¿Hola?"

"Mrs. Oliveira?"

"Yes?"

"It's Sandy."

"Oh, hi Sandy."

"Mrs. Oliveira, is Lareina staying with you for the weekend?"

"No, Sandy. Why?"

"She's not home. She hasn't been home since she left for her final exam yesterday."

"Really?! Are you sure? That's not like her. That is very odd."

"Yes, I know. I'm sorry to say it, but she hasn't been back here at all. I'm really worried about her."

"Have you tried calling her?"

"Uhhh...no. Not yet."

"Ok. I know this is out of character for her, but I think you should call her before we do anything extreme."

"Ok, Mrs. Oliveira. I will. Thank you. I will keep you up dated."

Lareina woke to feel the vibration of her cell phone in her pants pocket. Though she was still quite groggy, she knew that she had to try to get to her phone so she could get help. She tried, but she couldn't reach it. How she wished she could answer and have someone come and get her away from this insane man. Instead, the phone continued to vibrate until her voice mail answered. Lareina sighed. She knew that phone was her only link to getting help; she prayed that it wouldn't die before she could reach out to save her own life.

According to her call list, this was the tenth call Sandy was going to make to Lareina's cell phone, not to mention the several text messages she had sent. Sandy took a deep breath as she redialed the number. Again, after multiple rings, it went to Lareina's voice mail.

"Lareina, it's Sandy again. Look, your family and I are really worried about you.

"Where are you?! Please call or text us so we know you're ok."

Sandy hung up feeling completely defeated.

With a heavy sigh, she dialed the number for the Oliveiras.

"Hello, Mrs. Oliveira?"

"Yes. Hi, Sandy."

"Mrs. Oliveira, I have called Lareina at least ten times. I've sent her tons of text messages. She's not answering me. I'm really worried."

"She's not answering our calls either, Sandy. We are just as concerned."

"Oh no! She's not answering your calls either? Oh God! Ok, I'm calling the police, Mrs. Oliveira. I have to."

"Yes, Sandy. Please do. Tell me what happens; what they tell you."

"I will, Mrs. Oliveira. I promise."

38

Again, Lareina's cell vibrated. She knew it had to be Sandy, or her family or both. She desperately wanted them to come save her, but she had no way of communicating with anyone outside of Tony.

Tony was too engulfed by the heavy metal music he was playing to know what was going on in the back of the car.

A feeling of isolation began to overwhelm Lareina. She had to fight through it. She knew she had to be rational, sharp, and quick. She couldn't let her emotions take over. It was difficult as she lay on the floor, battling the tears and her fears.

Marcus Raymer sat at his desk and sighed as he stared off and let his mind wander. It was quiet today at work, the perfect opportunity for him to reflect on his life.

He had had another lonely, quiet night last night which lead into another lonely, quiet day today. Though not much of a people person, he did crave human companionship and interaction. He felt cut off from the rest of the world. He also felt like he was aging far beyond his years, and he had no one with whom to share his precious non-work time. His friends consisted solely of co-workers. His world - his entire existence - was completely contained at his desk.

Marc was a very handsome man. He had short light, sandy brown hair. His eyes were a soothing, rich deep brown. He worked out regularly (it was the only distraction he had from his loneliness) so his body was strong, lean and muscular. Beyond his attractive physical appearance, he knew he had a lot to offer the right person. But she seemed to be nothing more than a mere fairy tale. No one ever approached him, and he had yet to find someone who was of interest to him. Marcus' life was passing before him, and all he did – all he could do - was work. He simply worked as a Missing Persons detective; that seemed to be the only purpose to his life.

Marc was originally from England, but he had been living in the states for some time now. He loved the sun that California offered and that England so severely lacked.

He had worked as a British constable in London for a number of years, but after his parent's tragic deaths, he felt that England had nothing left to offer. His parents' unexpected deaths from an arson set fire were so traumatic for him that he knew it would be best to get away from the memories. Besides, the lure of the Southern California weather was far too great for him to resist.

So he left for America, to work as a police officer. America had given him everything he dreamed of – well, mostly anyway.

As he continued to wallow in deep reflection and self-pity his phone rang, jolting him back into reality.

"Detective Raymer, Missing Persons."

"Help me, please! My name is Sandy Taylor. My roommate, Lareina Oliveira, is missing."

"Ok, ok. Calm down. I'm going to ask you some questions, ok?

"First off, how old is she?"

"Thirty two."

"Ok. And how long has she been missing?"

"It's been well over twenty four hours. She left yesterday to take her final exam at UNLV, and hasn't come home."

"Have you found her vehicle?"

"No, sir. It's a 2003 Chevrolet S-10 king cab. It's black. She has a California license plate that reads, 'X is 2.'"

"Let me make sure I have that correct. That's x as in xylophone; the word is: i as in indigo and s as in Samuel; and the number two?" Marc wrote all of the information down on a small pad of paper. He wanted to be sure he didn't miss any details.

"Yes sir. Please help, I'm worried."

"Is it unusual for her not to come home?"

"Extremely." Sandy's voice quaked as she spoke to the detective.

"Now, you said she was taking a final exam at the University."

"Yes, she's a Ph. D. student. She was taking her final exam in algebra."

"Ummm, her professor is uhhh...Dr. Bauer.

"You have to find her, please! I've been calling and texting her for hours. She won't return calls to me or her family! Something's wrong, I just know it."

"Is there any potential that she decided to just take a break after her exam and take a weekend in solitude?

"Had she met anyone that she might just run to Vegas with them and get married and simply not tell anyone?"

"No, no! That's not her at all! She's extremely reliable. Her family means everything to her. And she's not dating anyone. She wouldn't just run away at thirty two! Something must have happened to her!"

"Ok, ok. Calm down. Do you know anyone who might be after her? Anyone who would want to purposely hurt her? Any angry ex-boyfriends or husbands or anything like that?"

"No, sir. No one. Everyone likes her: she's a very sweet, kind, caring person. She has no enemies, so to speak."

"Ok. Do you know of any angry friends, co-workers, teachers, or classmates? Anyone who displayed any unusual behavior?"

"Ummm...no, no. Not that I can think of. Not off the top of my head, anyway."

"Ok, well I want you to think of any and all possible people, and I'll start by going to investigate things over at the University.

"What is your number Miss Taylor?"

Sandy gave Detective Raymer her cell phone number. She hoped she could trust this man. She prayed that he would be able to bring Lareina home soon.

After a moment, Marcus then spoke. "Ok, write down this number. This is my cell phone number; you can reach me on it at any time." Detective Raymer gave Sandy his number slowly so she could write it down.

"Ok," Sandy sniffled into the phone.

"It's ok, Miss Taylor. We'll find Lareina."

"Ok, thank you."

At the University, Lareina's truck sat conspicuously in the nearly empty parking lot. Marc had the crime scene team finger print the truck and examine it. A police tow truck was en route to bring it back to the crime lab's garage for a more detailed inspection. Marc left the truck to go inside the school to try to find Dr. Bauer.

Just as Marc was entering the building, a tall woman passed him.

Marc stopped her. "Excuse me Miss, do you know where I could find Dr. Amanda Bauer?"

"I am Dr. Bauer, sir."

"Dr. Bauer, my name is Detective Marcus Raymer. I am from the Missing Persons department of the LAPD. One of your students has gone missing."

"One of my students?! What?! Are you sure? Who is it?!"

"It's Miss Lareina Oliveira, Dr. Bauer."

"Oh my God!"

"Was she in class to take her final exam yesterday?"

"Oh yes! Lareina is one of my best students. She was there, and finished the test in under an hour. She was the first to leave."

"Were all of the students in class for the final exam?"

"Ummm...everyone was there, save for one student. But, he was out of town for a family issue. He had already told me he would not be around, so he and I had rescheduled his test so he could go take care of his family. I'm not sure where he was, but he said it was far from LA.

"Had Lareina had any problems with any of her classmates that you know of?"

"No, Lareina didn't have any enemies or any problems with any other students. Well, not that I am aware of, anyway."

"Ok.

"And what is the name of the one student who was away?"

"Anthony Covelli."

Marc quickly scribbled all of this information into a tiny notebook he held in the palm of his large hand. "Is it possible that Mr. Covelli had a problem with Lareina?"

"I doubt it, detective. From what I saw, they hardly spoke."

"And no one in the class showed any odd behavior? Lareina included?"

"No. Everyone and everything seemed status quo."

"Dr. Bauer, Lareina's truck is still in the parking lot. Do you know if she was supposed to go out with anyone last night?"

"No. Lareina's an extremely studious person, and she works as a high school teacher. She didn't strike me as the type to party at all."

"Oh, ok.

"Do you know if she was having any car problems? Maybe a friend or acquaintance, or perhaps even a tow truck was supposed to come and help her?" Marcus was looking at every possible angle and scenario in order to put the pieces of Lareina's disappearance together.

"She's never mentioned any vehicle difficulties. She never seemed to have any problems with her truck in the past."

"Hmmm. Ok.

"Now, you said before that she was the first to leave after the test. How long was it from when she left to the next student?

"Oh, I don't know, Detective Raymer. Twenty, maybe twenty five minutes."

"That long? Hmmmm...ok.

"Well, thank you for your time, Dr. Bauer. Here's my card. Please call me if you can think of anything."

"Oh I will. Lareina's a great young woman. I hate to see anything happen to her. I'll call if I can think of anything."

"Thank you, Dr. Bauer."

Marc walked back towards Lareina's truck to see if the CSI team had found any information or possible leads. As people continued to swarm around the lone black truck, the tow truck had arrived.

The CSI team sealed all the doors and tailgate, and the truck was hauled off for further investigation. Now all signs of Lareina's presence on the campus had been erased.

She had been stuck in the back of the Mustang for a while. Lareina had no idea how long they had been driving as she was still a bit groggy from the drug Tony had given her last night. Heavy metal had been playing constantly as far back as Lareina's foggy memory could recall. It was haunting and frightening all at the same time. The songs were sung in a language that was quite foreign to Lareina. She couldn't understand them at all. Not understanding the lyrics only frightened Lareina more. As much as she fought to ignore it, the music penetrated her ears and overwhelmed her.

Trying to keep her wits about her, Lareina knew that she had to see where they were; to get some idea of where they were going. Slowly, quietly, Lareina wiggled her way forward so that she could take a peak out of the window.

She gradually raised her head, but not too high since she was right behind Tony's seat. They were inland, they had left the coast. No longer were there beaches or palm trees. She saw tall pine trees and various flora, but no landmarks or signs. She desperately prayed for some kind of sign. She felt as if she was truly in the middle of nowhere.

Miraculously, as her eyes scanned the outside world, she saw a sign. They were on Route CA 99 headed north.

Slowly, she lowered her head, and wiggled her way back down on to the floor. Route 99. She'd remember that. Somehow, someway, she'd let Sandy and her family know where she was. She refused to let Tony win. Silently, she lay on the floor of the car trying to plot clever ways of contacting people and ensure that she got rescued.

Marc sat down on the couch next to Sandy. "Do you have a picture of Lareina?"

"Yes, sir." Sandy jumped up and grabbed the most recent picture of her friend.

Marc looked at the picture. He was taken away by the young woman's stunning beauty. "She's gorgeous," he whispered.

"Yeah, she is." Sandy's reply brought Marc back to the immediate matter at hand, since his mind had been temporarily swept up by Lareina's striking image.

Marc looked up at Sandy. "Is it possible that someone is obsessed with her? A woman this beautiful could easily get a stalker or even multiple stalkers."

"Uhhhh, no. Not that I can think of, detective. I don't remember seeing people watching us. I mean, it's not like she'd leave class and her tires would be slashed or anything. There weren't any notes or anything like that. If she did have a stalker, neither one of us knew about it."

"There has to be someone with a motive, Miss Taylor.

"Does she or her family have money that perhaps someone would want a ransom?"

"Oh no. Absolutely not. They don't have that much. Well, they are comfortable, but they don't enough that anyone would go after them like that."

"You really can't think of anyone who would want to hurt her? Not one person with any kind of motive?"

"I have been wracking my brain all day, Detective. I swear, nothing's coming to mind.

"Lareina's always lived a good, simple life. We're both teachers. We never had any problems with anyone. I just can't understand who would want to do something like this - to hurt her." Sandy began to cry ceaselessly.

"It's ok, Miss Taylor. By any chance, have you spoken to her family?"

"Yes, sir."

"Are there any potential leads there? Have they seen or heard anything? Any family issues? Anything like that?"

"No, not at all. Consuelo and Jose couldn't think of anything."

"And who are Consuelo and Jose?"

"Lareina's parents, Detective. They said there were no rifts within the family, no known enemies. They can't think of anyone either."

"Well, if that changes - if anything does come to mind to you or to them, call me. I don't care if it's at two in the morning, just call me."

"Yes, Detective Raymer. I will."

Chapter 5

The Mustang finally stopped. Lareina stretched up to see her surroundings. They were stopped at a tiny little gas station in the middle of an opening surrounded by sky scraping trees. Tony started to get out of the car.

"Tony?" Lareina quietly spoke up.

He snapped around. "What?!"

"I'm sorry, but could you please cut the tape? I need to use the ladies' room. I'll be quick, I promise."

"I'll get the key for you first, and then come back to cut the tape on your wrists. That's it."

"That's fine. Thank you, Tony." Lareina was trying to be extra kind and tried to work with Tony's demands in the hopes it would help increase her chances to be freed. She waited several minutes for his return.

Tony returned to the car, with a scouring look on his face. He took out a very large knife, one that could easily cause significant harm to someone, and he cut the tape on her wrists, but he kept her ankles tied. "If you try anything, I'll use this on you," he threatened her.

"I promise I won't do anything funny. I'll be right back." Lareina pulled herself out of the car, and shuffled to the ladies' room. Once inside, she grabbed her cell phone from her pocket. There were countless calls and text messages from Sandy and her family.

Quickly, Lareina sent a text message to Sandy. "Route 99 north. Old, beat up red Mustang. Tony..." She was about to type in his full name when he pounded on the bathroom door.

"What the hell is going on in there?"

"I'm sorry, Tony. I'll be right there." She hit the send button, and then flushed the toilet so that Tony would believe her excuse. She ran the sink for an effect as if she were washing her hands.

Finally, her cell said that the message had sent. Lareina quickly turned the phone off and shoved it back in to her pocket. Quickly, she wet her hands, and came out.

Tony grabbed Lareina by the arm tightly as she came out. "Get back into the car! Now!"

Lareina shuffled back to the car as quickly as she could with her taped legs. She hopped into the car, and rolled onto the floor in the back. She didn't want to aggravate him any more than she already had.

Tony got into the driver's seat. With a grunt, he reached down and re-taped her wrists together tightly. It took a minute before the Mustang started back up. When it finally did, they continued to drive to Tony's special destination.

Marc was working out in his free time, as usual. Since he had nothing else to do, he decided he'd rather take care of his body than to sit alone in his empty apartment. Instead, he pushed his body to its physical limits at the precinct gym. It quelled his loneliness by keeping him busy.

Marc was alone in the gym as he bench pressed extremely heavy weights when he heard his cell phone had begun to ring.

"Shit," he said to himself. As carefully as he could, he brought the weights down, slid off the bench, and ran to pick up his cell.

"Detective Raymer."

"Hi Detective Raymer, it's Sandy Taylor."

"Well hello, Miss Taylor. Any news?"

"Yes, actually. I just got a text from Lareina."

"Really? Wow! That's a great sign. What does it say?"

"Well, it's a bit odd. It doesn't seem like a full message. All it says, 'Route 99 north. Old, beat up red Mustang. Tony...'

"I'm not sure I fully understand it, Detective."

"Well, my guess is, she's somewhere on California Route 99 headed north.

"At this point, we don't know if she's in an old, beat up Mustang or if that is supposed to be some kind of landmark.

"Now, who is Tony?"

"Tony? Tony? Hmmmm...I don't know. We don't work with anyone named Tony, and she never knew a Tony that I can recall – oh wait! Yes she did! Oh my God! I totally forgot about him!"

"Really?! Ummm...ok. So, now that you remember him, tell me everything you can about this guy."

"Well...uhhhh...Tony was a guy in her class. She said he was a bit creepy and seemed to have a thing for her, but he seemed harmless.

"I mean, he asked her out a few times, but that was all she ever told me about."

"Could he have had enough of a 'thing' for her that he'd do this?" Marc asked.

"Based on what she told me, he didn't seem like he was controlling or domineering. She just said he was weird."

"Well, weird can be enough. For now, it's what we'll have to go on.

"You said he was a classmate of hers?"

"Yes, sir."

"Ok, let me go call Dr. Bauer and see what she can tell me."

"I am so sorry I didn't remember him sooner, Detective."

"It's ok, Miss Taylor. You remembered now, so now we have a lead and I am going to check it out. I will keep working until we bring Lareina home."

The ride was bumpy now. It seemed to Lareina as though they were off the road, driving on very uneven terrain. The Mustang's engine could be heard straining to move the car forward over what felt to be rocks and dirt. Lareina pulled her head up as best she could. It was so dark, she could hardly see, and it seemed that all she could see were tall pine trees. As she peered out the window at the endless trees, she realized she really was Tony's prisoner in this vast, dark forest.

"Dr. Bauer?"

"Yes?" The voice on the other end was scratchy. He had clearly woken her.

"I'm sorry to disturb you at this time of night. This is Detective Raymer."

"Oh dear God! Detective! Any news?"

"Yes, but I have a few questions first.

"You said you had a man named Tony in the same class as Lareina?"

"Yes, sir. Yes I did."

"Ok, good. Now, I was just going through my notes. You said he was the only one not present at the final exam, right?"

"Yes, that is correct. He had taken the test early. He took it the week before everyone else. He said he needed to leave town the day of the final to help move his father to a nursing home. So, he and I scheduled it for an earlier date."

"Is there anyway we can validate his story?"

"I don't know. I don't think so, Detective. He didn't give me any details, so I doubt it.Although if you spoke to him directly, I'm sure he'd be happy to give you the information."

"Dr. Bauer, were there any other students named Tony in that class?"

"No, detective. Just Tony - Anthony Covelli, I should say."

"Tony Covelli? And that's spelled C- o- v- e- l- l- i?"

"Yes.

"Like I said, I'm sure that if you contacted him directly you could get the information you need."

"No, we can't, Dr. Bauer. He's our possible suspect."

Marc could hear her gasp in shock.

"Dr. Bauer, I'm going to need his information. Is it possible for you to have someone at the school fax over his school registration information? This city is too damn big for me to just look up Tony Covelli. I'll get far too many hits. I need his social - something more specific and detailed to go by."

"Yes, detective. I will call them first thing in the morning."

"Thank you, Doctor. I appreciate it. I will keep you posted on our progress."

"Please do, Detective Raymer. Lareina is a very special woman. I want to see her come home safely."

"We all do, Dr. Bauer."

The second night came to a close on Lareina's kidnapping, and there was still little to go on. Time was always of the essence in these cases, and time was not Marc's friend with this particular case so far. As he hung up, Marc hoped that it wasn't too late for the Latin beauty.

Tony grabbed Lareina and dragged her out of the car.

"Tony, where are we?"

"What does it matter?"

"Ummm...well, I'd just like to know, that's all." Lareina said as meekly and innocently as she could.

Tony sighed while he thought for a moment. "Well, it is your new home, so I guess it's ok. We're up by the Merced River, just north of Elephant Rock, over by Yosemite."

"Oh, ok. Thank you," Lareina's voice cracked as Tony tightened his grip on the back of her shirt.

Tony continued to drag Lareina through the forest until they came to an old, dilapidated cabin. Tony opened the door and threw her inside. Lareina hit the floor hard. It was too dark to see anything of her surroundings.

"How did you know about this place, Tony? This is really far from L.A."

"That doesn't matter to you.

"What does matter is that we're here. You're mine now, and no one else can have you. We'll stay here forever if that's what it takes. You belong to me."

Lareina was unsure how to respond to Tony's horrid controlling and domineering comments. She desperately wanted to argue back, but she knew it would only make things worse. She simply sighed out of fear and frustration. She moved slowly to try to prop herself up off from the hard, splintered floor.

"Stay where you are," Tony said, seeing that Lareina was struggling to move. "That's your bed for tonight. Get some sleep. You're going to need it."

Chapter 6

Marc looked over the school registration form sent to him by UCLA earlier that morning. Tony's full name, social security number and even his car information was listed. Under the car's description was listed a 1984 red Ford Mustang with California license plates.

Marc looked up the license plate number in the police data base. The plates were registered to Tony. Marc now figured that the part of Lareina's text about an "old beat up red Mustang" must have been about Tony's car.

He decided to put out a state-wide APB on Tony's Mustang. They had lost so much precious time already. Marc had to do as much as he could, and as quickly as he could in order to make up for it. All he could do was hope that Tony and Lareina were still in California, and that someone would see or recognize the car.

Marc picked up his phone and called Sandy to update her.

"Hello, Miss Taylor?"

"Yes?" Her voice was unsteady. She had clearly been crying.

"It's Detective Raymer."

"Oh hi, Detective."

"Miss Taylor, I do have a bit of some good news. We have information on Tony and his car.

"That bit about an old beat up Mustang in the text message referred to Tony's vehicle. We have just put out a state-wide all points bulletin on the car. Hopefully, someone will come up with something soon."

"So, you think it really is Tony?"

"Right now, he's the only lead we have. Unless and until he can account for his whereabouts, he is currently our prime suspect."

"Ok. So then what do we do in the meantime?"

"Well, there's nothing that you can do right now, but wait and let us work. You need to let us do our job. We're detectives, so let us detect, if you will. I will keep you posted of our progress, I promise."

"Wait?! I have to wait?! Are you kidding me?! She could be dead by now, Detective Raymer!" Sandy began crying into the phone.

"Look, Miss Taylor, I know this is extremely difficult for you.

"Why don't you call Lareina's family and Dr. Bauer? They all need to know everything that's going on as well. This way you're helping, and everyone is in the loop, ok?

"In the meanwhile, we're making up a missing person flier and some of the officers and I are going to blanket the city with them, ok?

"Trust me, I understand how difficult this situation is for you. I promise you that we're working on every possible aspect of this case. I need you to just trust us.

"If you get any more messages from her, though, please let me know immediately.

"Together, we'll get Lareina back. That's a promise."

Lareina had slept very little on the hard floor, but the sunlight beaming in through the old, faded windows made it impossible for her to get any further rest. Slowly, as she opened her eyes and attempted to sit up, she saw Tony in an old rocking chair watching her.

"Good morning, my dear," he greeted her in a creepy tone. Slowly, he stood up and approached her. There was a monstrous look in his eyes. "So, what should we do on this first day of our honeymoon?" He asked as he knelt down beside Lareina.

"Honeymoon?!" Lareina was sickened by the thought.

"Oh yes. Of course! You're mine now – you belong to me. And you always will. Just like in a marriage. Granted we didn't have a ceremony, but that's ok. You and I know it, and that's all that really matters.

"So, this would be like our honeymoon." Tony stood up and hovered over Lareina.

Lareina stared up at him, silently. She was unable to fully comprehend what he was saying.

"What to do, what to do." Tony said, yet there was an indication in his tone that he already had a plan. "Actually, come to think of it, we haven't even consummated our marriage yet!" Tony looked down at Lareina and there was a look in his eyes that caused her great fear.

"Wait, Tony! No, please don't!"

Tony cut the tape that bound her hands. He grabbed her arms, stretched them out over her head, and re-taped them. He began unbuttoning her blouse.

"No, Tony!" She pleaded. "Please, stop. Don't!"

"Sshhhh, you just don't know what you're saying. This will make our marriage official."

"No, Tony! Please, I'm begging you! I don't want to. I've never..."

"You've never what? What?!"

"Tony, please. I've never been with a man before. Please leave me alone!"

"No way! Are you kidding me?! You mean to tell me my beautiful bride is a virgin? It doesn't get any more perfect than that!"

Now, he hurried as he finished unbuttoning her blouse. He shoved it underneath her. He quickly unbuttoned her pants and slid them down. Fortunately, he did not feel the cell phone in her pocket. Her pants were bunched up around the tape on her ankles. That was enough for Tony. He had all the room he needed.

Lareina lay on the hard, dirty, dusty floor only in her panties and bra. She felt so helpless, so dirty, so embarrassed. This was not how her first time was supposed to be. She closed her eyes and prayed she'd wake from this nightmare.

Tony fumbled a bit, but finally unsnapped Lareina's bra; and then he pulled down her panties, exposing her beautiful, untouched body.

Lareina wanted to hide her nakedness in shame, so she turned her head away, still keeping her eyes closed. She prayed that if she didn't see it, it couldn't possibly be happening.

Rapidly, Tony pulled off his pants, and jumped on top of Lareina. He forced his fat self into her tense, nervous body.

"Oh, owe! That hurts! Please stop, Tony," Lareina begged while endless tears made their way down her face.

Tony did not regard her pleads, and he continued to enjoy himself while Lareina writhed in agony.

After an infinite torturous time, Tony finally finished.

As he stood up, there was blood on the floor, on her legs, and even on him. He looked at the mess.

"Damn it!" He screamed at the top of his lungs.

Lareina continued to look away so he wouldn't see her tears.

"God damn it, Lareina! Look at the mess you caused!" Tony grabbed Lareina's face and forced her to view the aftermath of his assault. "At least I know you weren't lying," he said, still holding on to her face. "Now, you truly belong to me. No one else can have that!

"I'll have to go find a town a store so we can clean up." He grabbed her panties and pants and quickly clothed her again. "Ok, now you look decent. We can't have my wife looking like a damn crack whore.

"I'll go get the cleaning supplies, ok? I'll be back soon. I love you."

Lareina simply grunted, and turned away from him again as tears continued to stream down her face.

Marc and countless other police officers went through all parts of Los Angeles. They created a large circular radius blanketing the greater Los Angeles area with fliers and checking for any possible leads in Lareina's kidnapping. They went as far north as Burbank; as far east as Baldwin Park; even as south as Compton, and as far west as Santa Monica. They handed out the fliers, asking if anyone had seen Lareina. They also posted the fliers anywhere and everywhere they possibly could. Soon, Lareina's face and information could be found all over Los Angeles.

No matter where they went, though, no one had seen or even heard of Lareina. Not one soul had seen the Mustang. There were no leads to be found. No calls had come in yet from the APB. Although the city was now saturated with Lareina's image and the information pertaining to her kidnapping, they still had no way of finding the young woman.

As the hours in the day ticked away, Marc tried desperately to remain optimistic that they would be able to find her.

Lareina lay on the floor crying. She felt so dirty, so used. Her own body disgusted her because Tony had touched her. He had been inside of her! She cringed at the thought: she nearly vomited at that realization. As overwhelmed as she was by emotion, she suddenly became aware of the fact that this was a prime opportunity to take advantage of her solitude.

With great difficulty, she wriggled and moved so that her arms were no longer above her head. The tape on her wrists gave her very limited hand movement. She pulled her knees up so she could try to reach her cell phone. It took countless attempts, but she was finally able to grab it.

Lareina fought to turn the phone on. After several tries, she was able to manipulate her hands and fingers to get the phone to work. It had minimal signal. She knew she couldn't expect much: they were in the middle of the forest, far from civilization.

Lareina struggled, but she was able to turn on the phone's GPS. She then tried to type a text message to Sandy. "My GPS is on. Try to find my location. Please hurry!"

After quite a few minutes, the message finally sent. The phone still held a full charge, so she turned all vibrations and sounds off, but left the phone on, in the hopes that the GPS signal would lead someone to her rescue.

As quickly as she could, Lareina wrestled to put the phone back neatly in her pocket so Tony wouldn't suspect anything. Then she moved and wiggled her way back into the same position she was in when Tony left.

Lareina fought to breathe. The emotion and intensity of the day were overwhelming her. She prayed that her plan would work.

Now, all she could do was quietly wait for her perpetrator's return.

Chapter 7

Hours had passed, and yet Tony still hadn't returned. The sun sat low in the sky, and the old cabin glowed in a late afternoon orange luminescence. "Where could he be?" Lareina wondered. She didn't want him near her, but she also knew that if he never returned she had little possibility of surviving. Concern and fear washed over her.

She decided to check her phone. Knowing the tricks to moving around now, Lareina was able to manipulate her body much more easily this time.

She pulled the phone out of her pocket. There were no calls, no text messages, no responses to her message at all. Her battery had lost some power. Not knowing how much longer she would be stuck as Tony's prisoner, Lareina reluctantly turned her phone off. She sighed heavily. She had so greatly hoped that her GPS text and signal would bring her salvation, but it only brought silence.

Sadly, she slipped the phone back in her pocket and assumed her original position. All she could do now was hope that Tony would return soon, or that someone would come and find her.

About thirty minutes after Lareina's last cell phone escapade, Tony returned to the cabin. He came inside with a few grocery bags.

"Hi, honey. I'm home." He laughed out loud at himself. He was so proud of himself. What a perfect little life he was building in the abandoned cabin. "Sorry I was gone for so long," he said placing the bags down. "There are no towns close to where we are. It took me a while to even find a place!

"I got us some food and necessities, though."

Lareina wiggled to sit up. "Food!" she thought to herself. She was dying to eat.

"And I bought bleach to clean up your mess from this morning.

"You don't get any food until you clean that spot up perfectly, do you hear me?"

Lareina remained silent.

"I said you don't get any food until you clean up your mess perfectly! Do you understand me?!" Tony yelled at the top of his lungs. His unpredictable behavior was terrifying to Lareina.

"Yes," she mumbled.

Tony threw a bottle of bleach and a scrubbing brush at her.

"Clean it up! NOW!"

With great difficulty, Lareina opened the bleach bottle. Unable to fully grasp it because of her hands being bound, bleach spilled all over the old, dry, wooden floor.

"Damn it! Do I have to do everything around here?! You can't even open a fucking bottle of bleach?! What the hell is wrong with you?!" Tony screamed at her.

Lareina took a deep breath. The smell of the undiluted bleach was extremely potent and she began to cough.

Tony kicked the scrub brush towards her.

"I want all of this clean, and I want it done now." He retreated to the rocking chair she had found him in earlier that day, so he could watch and be sure that she cleaned up the mess to his high expectations.

She grabbed the brush as best she could, and scrubbed the floor, while on her hands and knees. She scrubbed the spot of blood as best she could until it finally faded away into the old, brittle wood. She continued to scrub the floor until all of the spilled bleach had dissipated.

"Good, that's more like it," Tony sneered.

Sandy looked at her beeping phone. There was another text message from Lareina! Sandy sighed out of relief. There was still hope that she was alive. Sandy opened the message. It read, "My GPS is on. Try to find my location. Please hurry!"

Sandy immediately called Marc Raymer.

"Detective Raymer."

"Detective, it's Sandy Taylor."

"Hello, Miss Taylor. Do you have any news?"

"Yes! Lareina sent me another text message. She's still alive!"

"That's great! It's wonderful news! What does the message say?"

"'My GPS is on. Try to find my location. Please hurry!'"

"That's great! She's smart. Turning on her GPS means that we could get to her within a matter of just a few hours.

"What is the time stamp on the message?"

"Let me look. Uhhhh...it looks like it was from 7:03 this morning."

"Shit! Miss Taylor, it's ten o'clock at night! We don't know if her GPS is still on, if she is in a specific location or they're still traveling"

"I'm sorry, detective. I really am. But, I only just received the message now."

"What's her number?"

"What?"

"What is Lareina's cell number?" Marc asked with obvious impatience.

Sandy had Lareina's number on speed dial, so it took her a few moments to look it up and give Marc the number.

"Ok, let me see if we can still get a hold of the GPS, or at least see where she was this morning. I'll call you back."

Marc hung up. "Damn it!" He said out loud to himself.

With a sigh, he called upstairs to Brian to see about tracking her number by finding her GPS signal.

"No, Marc," Brian said. "I'm sorry but I don't see a current signal coming from that phone."

"Shit. Brian, can you go back and trace the GPS from this morning?"

"Yeah, Marc. I can. But it's going to take me some time. I'll call you back."

"Thanks, Brian."

Marc waited anxiously for Brian to call back. None of their fliers had turned up any leads, and tomorrow Marc had to hold a press conference with the Chief about the case in the hopes that it would create more leads. "Damn it," Marc thought. "I have to find this girl!"

After quite some time had passed, the phone on Marc's desk rang.

"Yeah?"

"Marc, it's Brian. I have some bad news."

"What is it?"

"The GPS was coming from somewhere way north and east of Los Angeles. It's South of Yosemite, but it's in an extremely heavily wooded area. There are lakes and rivers all around. I couldn't pinpoint it at all."

"Not at all, Brian?"

"No. Sorry, Marc."

"Damn!" Marc paused to take a deep breath. "Brian, can you at least give me a general area?"

"Anywhere from Fresno all the way east to Yosemite."

"Are you fucking kidding me?"

"No, I'm sorry, Marc. I think she's still pretty east of Fresno based on what I see here, but that's the best that I can do."

"Thanks, Brian." They hung up. "She could be anywhere, and she's at least five hours away - and that's only if they have settled on a location," Marc thought. "Fuck!" He cried out into the empty office. He looked at the picture of the beautiful Lareina. "I'm sorry, Lareina. We'll find you. I don't know how, but we'll find you. Stay sharp, stay strong. We're going to save you, I promise."

It was very late at night when Lareina and Tony finally ate.

"See, wasn't that a nice dinner, honey? Do you see all the nice things I do for you? I am such a good husband!"

Lareina tried to hide her disgust.

Tony had bought a tank of propane so that they could cook. He simply heated some cheap hot dogs he bought while he was out during the day.

The one good thing that came with dinner was that Tony had released Lareina from both her hand and ankle bindings.

"I'm even going to be so nice that I'll wash everything in the lake and let you stay here without being tied up. I am so nice to you! Damn, I am such a good husband." Tony stood up and gathered all the dishes.

Lareina knew this could be her one and only chance to escape.

With the two plates and a pair of forks in hand, Tony turned away to walk out the door. Lareina stepped as lightly as she could behind him. Step by step, she inched her way closer to the fat man. When she was close enough, she leaped forward and jumped on his back.

The plates and forks went flying out of Tony's hands and crashed down to the floor.

Lareina quickly covered Tony's eyes so that he couldn't see.

The two moved around and wrestled. Tony spun around endlessly trying to make Lareina dizzy. He tried pulling her delicate hands off his eyes, but her determination was great. She had a strong grip on him – far stronger than he expected. After swirling around the room with the small woman on his back, Tony leaned forward. Still trying to hold onto his face, Lareina began to lose her grip. She gripped his fat body with her legs as best she could. Her body was wrapped tightly over him.

Unexpectedly, Tony was able to wiggle an arm free and he grabbed her arm and was able to throw her forward. Lareina flew in the air a few feet before she finally landed on the hard floor on her back.

Tony came up from behind her and kicked her in the ribs three times. "Is this what you want?" He screamed as he kicked her. "Well, is it?!"

Lareina simply grunted from the pain.

Tony next grabbed her hair and pulled her entire body up by her hair.

Still reeling from her back pain, Lareina turned uncomfortably so she could see Tony's face. She saw that he was about to punch her in the face. She ducked down quickly. Using her stance to her advantage, she punched him in his groin.

Tony bent forward from the pain, but he stared straight at her. With an intense anger in his eyes, still bent forward, he charged her and pushed her down again.

Lareina slid backwards a bit, feeling the old wood floor scratch and splinter her back. Without missing a beat, Lareina jumped right back onto her feet. She steadied herself and then charged back at Tony. She ran into him using her shoulder for strength and leverage. She was shocked to see that she had only pushed him back a few feet.

She started to run at him again when he pulled the large knife out from his pocket. Lareina stopped dead in her tracks. The two stood staring at each other, with only a few feet between them.

"Wanna play?" Tony's voice sounded like pure evil.

He lunged forward but Lareina was able to jump back, unscathed.

She watched warily as Tony moved around the room. She leaned forward as he started coming at her from her left side. She quickly ran to the right, grabbed his fat arm from behind and pulled it up behind his back. Tony screamed out in pain.

Lareina pulled his arm up again with all of her might, in order to inflict more pain. He screamed again. Lareina knew she had him in a good position, but she couldn't figure out how to completely incapacitate him so she could protect herself.

Still holding his arm up behind his back, Lareina kicked Tony in the back. Once again, he screamed out in pain. She felt him buckle in her hand.

Thinking that he was weak enough, she tried to pull his arm up one last time, but her hands slipped, and he was suddenly free.

Tony quickly turned around. He grabbed Lareina's thin arm and spun her around so her back was pressed against his portly abdomen. Before she even realized what had happened, he had the knife pressed strongly against her neck.

"You won't win this one, honey," Tony scorned her. He pressed the knife against her jugular even harder. "Don't do this again, or I will kill you." He pushed her forward, and Lareina fell onto the floor on her hands and knees. She could feel her hands and knees were cut up and splintered from the floor. She dare not look at her wounds. She simply stayed there until Tony returned with the electrical tape.

Tony pulled her up by her elbow. Quickly, he wrapped the tape around her arms several times. He then repeated the pattern for her ankles.

"Just for that, you sleep on the floor again tonight. And to think, I bought blankets just for you. Oh well, I'll just use them." Tony dragged Lareina to the area where she had slept the previous night, and left her there to try to rest after their battle.

"I want to thank everyone for coming today," Chief Karl Hamilton said. "We have a missing person, and we believe her life to be in grave danger. I'll allow lead Detective Marcus Raymer to explain more about this case."

Marc stepped up to the podium. "Thank you, Chief Hamilton.

"Lareina Oliveira went missing two days ago from the UCLA campus. She is a Ph. D. student there, and we believe that one of her classmates may have abducted her.

"Ms. Oliveira is of Hispanic origin. She has black, shoulder length hair, and tan olive skin. Her eyes are hazel. She is stands at five feet even, and weighs about one hundred and five pounds.

"Our suspect is a man named Anthony Covelli. Mr. Covelli is Caucasian. He has curly, dark brown hair, and a matching goatee. Mr. Covelli is five foot eight, and weighs around three hundred and ten pounds.

"Mr. Covelli owns a red 1984 Ford Mustang. We have reason to believe that he taken Miss Oliveira in that car. The license plates are from California, and the plate number is '159 CRS3.'

"Our latest information tells us that they are still somewhere in the state of California. We are asking everyone in the Los Angeles area, as well as everyone state-wide to please help us in apprehending Mr. Covelli and saving Miss Oliveira.

"That is the latest information we have. If anyone has any new or pertinent information, please call the TIPS line. Thank you."

Marc stepped away as the Chief took some questions from the media. He sighed heavily, hoping that this press conference would somehow bring Lareina home.

Chapter 8

Once again, the sun beams came through the window and woke Lareina. She looked up to find Tony staring at her yet again.

"Good morning sleepy head.

"I have decided that since it's been a few days and since we have no running water, I think it's best that we go wash you and your clothes in the river."

Lareina's jaw dropped.

"Don't worry, honey. You'll feel nice and clean after all this," Tony said with a snicker.

Lareina's thoughts immediately went to her cell phone. Somehow, she needed to hide it. But where? How? Suddenly, an idea came to her.

"Ummm, ok. But, may I please be released so that I can go to the bathroom before we go?"

"I don't see why not." Tony stood up, walked over to Lareina, and cut the tape around her hands.

"I'm sorry, but my ankles too."

"Normally, I wouldn't mind doing that, but after last night I'm not sure that's such a good idea."

"I won't run away or do anything bad, Tony. I promise."

Tony stood above her, considering the consequences of releasing her ankles. He had done it every other time she asked to relieve herself. Finally, after several minutes of very heavy consideration, he decided to take a chance and cut her ankle ties.

"Thank you," she said softly.

Tony followed closely behind her as she walked outside. She turned to the left after stepping off the cabin porch, just as she had always done. She didn't want Tony to suspect that anything was different.

Tony continued straight down to the river, and waited for her. Lareina quickly found a tree that she hadn't used before, and that she would easily be able to find later. She went behind it, so Tony couldn't see her. She placed her cell phone down on the frozen ground; and she waited for a few minutes to fool him into thinking that she was in fact using the tree for other purposes.

She took in a deep breath, and tried to be brave as she walked back down towards the river, and towards Tony.

"That's a good girl," Tony said as she approached.

Nervously, she continued to move towards him.

"Take off your clothes," he demanded as she reached the river bank.

Lareina looked at the ground beneath her. How she desperately wished she didn't have to follow his commands. Slowly, she unbuttoned and unzipped her pants, and pulled them down. She followed suit with her underwear, blouse and bra. She stood in front of Tony embarrassed, naked, and uncomfortable.

"Good. Now, get in the water."

Lareina stood in place.

"I said, get in the God damn lake now!"

She walked into the river with trepidation, and allowed the cold river water to consume her.

Tony undressed himself, grabbed all their clothes, and came into the lake with her. He handed her the bunch of clothing. "Wash these."

Lareina sighed as she grabbed the clothes. She dunked them all into the water, and began to rub the material together. They had no soap, this was the only way she knew how to clean the clothes. She prayed it was to his liking.

"Scrub them harder." Her prayers weren't enough: Tony was clearly not pleased.

Lareina tried to appease Tony, but she seemed to be failing miserably.

"Harder! Scrub them harder, damn it! Get these fucking clothes clean!"

Lareina hand washed and scrubbed the clothes with what little energy she had, but it was not enough for Tony. He came up from behind her, grabbed the clothes out of her hands, and threw them onto the river bank.

Tony then grabbed her hair and shoved her face under the bitterly cold water.

Lareina began to struggle. Tony held her face down longer, and with greater force. Lareina was running out of air. Just as she began to fear that she was going to drown, Tony pulled her head up with great strength. Lareina gasped for breath, and Tony shoved her face back down into the cold abyss.

Again, she struggled. She moved and tried to loosen Tony's grip on her hair, but it was to no avail. She began to run out of air again. Once more, Tony pulled her head up just in time.

Lareina took in the biggest breath she could as her face was forced into the cold water yet again. This time, she did not struggle in the hopes that it would have her air supply last longer. The cold water harshly pierced her face as she tried to hold her breath for as long as possible. Finally, after a cold eternity Tony pulled her up again. Lareina fought to breathe normally again. Tony pulled back on her hair, and Lareina stumbled backwards in the water. It took her a few moments, but she finally regained her stability.

"Now you see what I'm truly capable of. Don't you dare ever make me do this again! I don't want to, but I'm not afraid to do whatever I have to." His hot breath fell on her ear. "I don't think you really understand what's going on here. You will do as I say, or I will kill you. There are no two ways about it. Get it?

"You will also never get away from me. Don't even think about it. If I can't have you, no one can. You belong to me, and you always will. Is that clear?"

With the little slack she had from his grasp on her hair, Lareina nodded her head yes.

"Good. Now go grab the clothes. They have dirt on them again. Clean them, and this time clean them well."

Still struggling to catch her breath and trying to slow her racing heart, Lareina walked up to retrieve the clothes. As she walked forward, she noticed an especially large, unique looking tree behind the cabin that could easily be seen from a hiking path. Somehow, she would have to use that tree to her advantage.

Keeping her newly discovered treasure a secret, Lareina picked up the clothes and re-entered the bitingly cold lake to do as she had been told.

Marc drove up the lonely highway. There weren't any other cars in sight. The ride was long and boring. He had left early this morning, since it was about a five hour drive to Fresno. He was on his fifth cup of coffee, trying very much to stay awake. Marc's fatigued was increased by the fact that he hadn't slept at all last night, either: he was too worried about this missing woman.

He saw yet another small gas station up ahead. There had been so many he had seen and stopped into along the way thus far and yet none had any information about Lareina's kidnapping. Pessimistically, he pulled into this station. He grabbed one of the fliers from the passenger seat with Lareina's picture and information on it. Despairingly, he walked into the store.

"Can I help you?" The clerk was a young boy, perhaps not even a college student yet.

"Yes, actually you can. My name is Detective Raymer. I'm from the LAPD's Missing Persons Department."

"This young lady went missing from UCLA three days ago. We have reason to believe that her kidnapper took her somewhere up this way. Have you seen her?"

"No, sir. I haven't. I'm sorry."

"We believe she was abducted in a red 1984 Mustang. Have you seen any cars like that in the past few days?"

"Ummm, let me think. We get so few customers, and the ones that aren't regulars tend to stick out in my mind.

"Wait. Ya know what? Come to think of it, yeah I did see one. It was an old red Mustang."

"You did?! Ok, now this is of the utmost importance. Do you happen to remember what the license plate number was?"

"No, sir. I'm sorry, but I don't keep track of stuff like that. Not unless I'm being robbed."

"Ok then, what can you tell me?" Marc asked, his heart was racing with anticipation.

"The guy came in, paid for some gas, and asked for the key to the bathroom, and that was it."

"Was anyone with him?"

"No, not that I saw."

"Can you describe him?"

"Ummmm...he was kind of short and pudgy, as I recall. He had really thick curly hair, and a thick goatee."

Marc was fairly sure that depiction fit Tony. He wrote the clerk's description in his small notepad. Every tiny bit of information was crucial at this point. "Did he happen to tell you where he was going or ask for any directions?"

"No, Detective. I'm sorry. I didn't really talk to him.

"Like I said he just paid for his gas, used the bathroom, and that was it. He couldn't have been here more than ten or fifteen minutes at the most. Sorry."

"No, that's actually really helpful. Thank you.

"Please, take this flier, and place it in the window. We have to find her."

"Oh, absolutely, Detective!" The young man took some tape, and quickly placed the flier in a predominant place in the store window.

"Thank you for your time. Here's my card if you see or hear anything, call me immediately."

"I sure will, Detective!"

Marc walked out of the store partially feeling positive since there had been a sighting, but also defeated since they still could not pinpoint Lareina's location.

He got back into his car, and called the Chief. "Hey Karl, it's Marcus."

"Hi Marcus. Whaddya got?"

"Well, there was a sighting on CA 99 just after the merge with Route 41. But, that's all it was. There is no indication as to exactly where they went."

"Shit! Well, at least it was a sighting. You're clearly on the right path, but we need something more solid to go on."

"Yeah, I know. I'm going to continue here, go into Fresno, and perhaps even go up into Yosemite. We at least need to get the word out up there."

"Sounds like a good plan. Keep me posted, Marcus."

"I will, Chief. Talk to you later."

Marc continued north, hoping that this would be the first of many sightings of Tony and/or Lareina. He knew he was close, and he simply wanted to bring her home as soon as possible.

Lareina sat in the cabin, wrapped up in a blanket, but she was still naked while the clothes dried on the porch railing. She still had yet to retrieve her cell phone. She shivered under the blanket from the cold that penetrated deeply into her bones.

Tony walked back into the cabin from the woods. His fat, ugly, naked body in front of Lareina. "Hi honey." He kissed her on the cheek. Lareina shuddered.

"You know, I bought a deck of cards yesterday. I think we should play a game."

Lareina looked at the floor. She loathed her existence here, and now Tony was going to force her to play a card game. She'd have to pretend to be happy, to somehow fake enthusiasm while playing a game. She hated the idea. She hated the situation. Lareina detested all that was Tony.

"Do you know how to play poker? Gin rummy?"

"Rummy," Lareina mumbled.

"Ok then! Rummy it is! Let me grab the cards, and we'll play. This will be so much fun!" Tony walked passed Lareina.

She sat, still looking at the floor, trying to understand the demented mind of Tony. She still could not predict his behavior. One minute he was threatening her. The next, he was trying to be sweet or act as if this was a normal situation. She couldn't figure out what may or may not trigger his anger. His emotions seemed so uncontrolled and irrational. His lack of predictability greatly frightened Lareina.

Tony returned far too quickly for Lareina, with the deck of cards in hand.

Lareina sighed heavily and she tried to feign an interest in their card game.

Marc walked into the Fresno police department.

"Can I help you, sir?" A uniformed officer asked as Marc entered.

"I hope so. My name is Detective Marcus Raymer. I am with the LAPD Missing Persons Department. We have a Los Angeles resident who was abducted and we have reason to believe she is near here. May I speak to your Chief about the case, please?"

"Oh sure, Detective. Just give me one minute, please."

The young officer disappeared into the back part of the building. Marc waited impatiently.

Finally, the officer returned with an older man.

"I'm in charge here. What can I do for you?" The older man asked. His tone was curt and cold.

"Sir, my name is Detective Marcus Raymer. I'm with the LAPD's Missing Persons department.

"We had an abduction three days ago. We have reason to believe that the suspect took this woman somewhere up in this area.

"Have you seen or heard of any unusual activity lately?"

"No, Detective. I'm sorry."

"Here's the flier. It has all of the information on both the missing woman and the suspect."

The scruffy police Chief looked at the flier for a moment. "Covelli?"

"Yes, sir. Anthony Covelli. Why?"

"Well, a few years ago, we had a case of child molestation by a Dominick Covelli."

"Really?" Marc was intrigued. Though Covelli is a common surname, Marc knew that sociopathic behavior like that is often found in several members of the same family. Marc hoped there could be a possible tie. He listened to the chief with great interest.

"Yes. It was horrendous, absolutely horrendous. It was one of my worst cases. Something I'll never forget. But like I said, his name was Dominick, not Anthony."

"Hmmmm...it could be a relation, or it could just be coincidence."

"It's hard to know, Detective."

"Yeah, it is.

"Thanks for the information, Chief.

"Anyway, the LAPD has put out a state-wide APB, but we haven't gotten any information. No leads, no tips, nothing. That's why I'm here. I was hoping that by actually coming up here, I could find some leads, and help to get other departments working with us."

"Certainly, Detective. Is your direct number on here?"

"No, not on the flier, sir. But here's my card. If you see or hear anything, please let me know immediately."

"We will."

"Thank you for your time and assistance, Chief..."

"Oh, I'm sorry. I forgot to introduce myself. I'm Chief Fred Wilmont."

"Ok, great. Thank you, Chief Wilmont."

Marc walked out of the building. He got back into his car and decided to head east. He wasn't sure what he'd find, if anything. It was worth a look.

The clock in his car read 4:05 pm. It was getting late. He had to hurry before it became too dark. The night in Yosemite was blindingly dark. Marc would be lucky if he could see his hand in front of his face. Knowing that time was against him, Marc headed out east as quickly as possible.

For the first time, Tony allowed Lareina to sleep on a blanket; and he also placed a blanket over her tonight as well. It wasn't much better than sleeping on the cold, hard floor, but she was grateful that it was at least something.

Tony came up and lay right next to her. "See isn't this cozy? We'll get to sleep next to each other every day for the rest of our lives like this."

Lareina felt nauseas at the thought, but she kept her opinion to herself.

Tony wrapped his paunchy body around Lareina and soon fell asleep.

Lareina lay awake trying to figure out ways of retrieving her cell phone from underneath the tree, and how she could get herself rescued as soon as possible.

Another long night passed as thoughts and ideas raced through Lareina's mind. Getting out alive was Lareina's one and only priority. Losing sleep to save herself was a small price to pay for her freedom.

Chapter 9

It was nearly midnight when Marc began his trek back home to Los Angeles, and he still had a drive of over fiver hours ahead of him. He was exhausted. Although it was late, he decided to call Sandy.

"Hello?" Her voice sounded tired and stressed.

"Miss Taylor, it's Detective Raymer."

"Oh, Detective. Please tell me you have some good news."

"Well, there was a sighting up on the way to Yosemite, but it was the only lead I found today.

"We do have one other thing to look into when I get back into the city."

"What's that?"

"Apparently there's a man named Dominick Covelli. He's had charges of child molestation brought up against him."

"What would that have to do with anything in Lareina's disappearance?"

"Well, if he's related to Tony, we might get a better lead or get some more information than what we have so far."

"Like as far as special family places, family history, or something?"

"Exactly, Miss Taylor.

"In the meanwhile, I want you to send a message to Lareina."

"You do? Why?"

"Yes. Since we missed the GPS attempt, I want you to send her a message with my number. Tell her to call me or send me a text message. If she can call, tell her to just leave the phone

Unbreakable Hostage

on. We can find her that way by her phone's GPS signal, and Tony wouldn't even know that we're tracking her."

"Oh! Wow, what a great idea! I would never have thought of that."

"Miss Taylor, this is of the utmost importance, so we need you to message her as soon as possible."

"Ok. I'll send that to her right now. Anything to bring her home."

"Good. I'll keep you posted on our progress, Miss Taylor."

"Thank you so much, Detective."

"You're welcome. Good night, Miss Taylor."

Marc hung up, and continued on his endless, dark drive.

Sandy immediately sent a text message to Lareina. In the text, Sandy gave Lareina Marc's number and told her to call or text him, and if possible to leave her cell on so the police could track her. Sandy then hit the send button. All she could do was hope and pray that Lareina would receive the message quickly, and that she would return home soon.

It was morning once again. Tony's thick body was still wrapped around Lareina. Gently, slowly, cautiously, she slipped out from underneath him. Thankfully, she didn't disturb him; he continued to sleep.

Lareina ran outside to get her phone by the tree. It was cold. She tried to warm it up in her hands, knowing it wouldn't work well if it was too cold. She turned it on. Slowly, the phone came up.

Lareina looked back at the cabin to see if anything was going on. She saw no movement or shadows, so it seemed that Tony was still sleeping. Lareina figured she still had a bit of time. She noticed that her phone hadn't received any messages from Sandy or her family. Lareina checked for messages a few times, but nothing showed up. She prayed they hadn't given up on her.

78

Quickly, she looked up her GPS. According to the GPS, her position was north thirty seven degrees, forty four minutes; west one hundred nineteen degrees and approximately forty minutes. As fast as she could, she wrote out a text message to Sandy. "X = 37° 44' and Y = 119° ~ 40'. Please get me!" She hit the send button. Her phone had very little signal. At least a full minute had passed while her phone tried frantically to pick up a signal and send out the message. Finally, her message had been sent.

Lareina turned off her phone, and ran back to the cabin. She put on her clothes which were still cold and damp. She then hid the phone back in her pants pocket. She entered the cabin just as Tony was beginning to wake up. She quickly started folding his clothes so as to fool him. The last thing Lareina wanted was for Tony to ever find out about her cell and her messages for help.

"Good morning," she tried to say as cheerfully as possible. "I hope you don't mind, I took the liberty of folding your clothes for you."

"Not at all," Tony yawned. "That's what you're supposed to do. What a good wifey!"

"Thank you. I'm trying." Lareina replied, though she was disgusted by this facade.

"What would you like for breakfast?"

"Oh, umm...I'm not really hungry right now."

Tony leaped up, and the knife suddenly appeared in his hand. "I asked you what you wanted for breakfast, not whether or not you were hungry.

"You will do as you are told: you will eat when I tell you to eat."

"But Tony I'm not..."

"No. Stop arguing! There is no debating this. Things will go as I say. Just to teach you - so that you fully understand, I'm going to give you a permanent reminder." Tony took the knife and slid it across Lareina's forearm.

The cut was long: it ran along the top of her forearm. Lareina noticed it was also somewhat deep. This injury would leave a large scar. Lareina's arm began bleeding heavily. She put her hand over the cut to try to stop the bleeding, but drops continued to flow down her arm and hit the floor. She looked at Tony with panic in her eyes.

"That will teach you." He walked away. Lareina stood in place, bleeding and fearing what Tony might do next.

A few minutes later, Tony returned from the kitchen with bleach, the scrub brush, tissues, and a rolled up bandage. "Clean and wrap up your damn arm. Then scrub the floor perfectly clean while I make breakfast. Is that understood?"

Lareina just looked at him.

"Is that understood?!"

"Yes," Lareina said in a defeated tone.

Tony walked away into the kitchen.

Lareina grabbed the tissues, and began wiping the blood off her arm. She tried to clean it as best she could with out any kind of soap or cleaner. She took the rolled bandage Tony had given her, and wrapped up her arm with as much pressure as she could create using only one hand. Her hopes were that she would quickly stop the bleeding.

Once she was satisfied with her bandage, she grabbed the bleach and the brush. With much disdain towards Tony, Lareina slowly got down and knelt on the floor. She poured small amounts of the bleach wherever she could find drops on the floor, and she scrubbed them out of the dry, brittle wood floor with all her might.

It was late afternoon when Marc's cell rang. "Detective Raymer."

"Detective, it's Sandy Taylor."

"Hello, Miss Taylor. Any news?"

"Yes, she's still alive. Thank God! I got another text from Lareina. But, I don't understand it."

"How do you mean?"

"It's all letters, numbers and symbols. I can't explain it. Can I show it to you?"

"Yes, absolutely. Give me a few minutes, and I'll be right over."

Marc had not taken the late afternoon Los Angeles traffic into consideration. He finally arrived at Sandy's house about forty five minutes later.

"I'm sorry it took me so long to get here, Miss Taylor. As usual, the traffic was horrendous."

"It's fine, Detective. I'm just glad you're here." Sandy brought her phone over to him. "Look."

Marc read the message, "X = 37° 44' and Y = 119° ~ 40'. Please get me!"

"It's some kind of algebraic formula, I think," Sandy said.

"I – I don't know, Miss Taylor. I'm not sure what that is or what it means. I've never seen a message like this before. I'm going to have to call Dr. Bauer and see if she has any idea what this means."

"But, it is a good sign. Like you said, it means she is alive. She must still have some battery power left in her phone as well."

"Please tell me you can find her."

"If we can figure this out quickly she may be home in a matter of hours, Miss Taylor. Please, just give me time to decipher this."

"Please hurry, Detective. I am worried sick about Lareina."

"As am I – we all are. And we will work as quickly as humanly possible, Miss Taylor." Marc wrote down exactly what the text message said. He bid farewell to Sandy, and left.

From his car, he called Dr. Bauer. She didn't answer, so he left her a voice mail.

"Dr. Bauer, this is Detective Raymer. We received a new text message from Lareina. We believe it to be some form of algebraic equation. We need your help deciphering this. Please call me immediately so we can bring Lareina home. Thank you."

Marc drove back to the station so that he could try to figure out this coded message.

Marc studied and studied the message. He never left the station that night. He worked all night trying to figure Lareina's code. "Talk to me, Lareina. Tell me what this means; where you are. Not everyone speaks math. Help me to help you," Marc whispered to himself.

He stared at the cryptic note endlessly.

Dr. Bauer had never called.

Yet another night fell, and while Marc worked endlessly to understand Lareina's message and she was still nowhere to be found.

Lareina's arm had been throbbing throughout the night. Thankfully, Tony was sleeping deeply and Lareina was able to move around. She walked over to the old, cracked and faded window. She looked out at the endless trees, the crescent moon and stars twinkling in the black sky.

Lareina examined her pounding arm. Some blood had leaked through her bandage. It was still wrapped tightly, and it seemed to be as secure as it could be considering what little she had been given to treat herself.

With a heavy sigh, she looked back out the window and wondered if she'd ever be found. She wondered if she would be stuck with this insane man forever; if he would truly kill her, or if she would be miraculously rescued. There was nothing, and no one around. Lareina began to strongly doubt that she would ever be rescued. She stared at the tranquil scene outside the window for several minutes. How she yearned to have that same peace and tranquility in her own heart. Instead she was living in anxiety and fear, and she hated it.

Feeling completely defeated, Lareina walked back to the blanket, and laid back down. She eventually resolved herself to this life in the cold, empty cabin, sleeping on the floor; the rest of the world thinking she simply fell off the face of the Earth. Unable to shake that morbid thought, she closed her eyes and tried to get some sleep.

Marc was startled when his desk phone rang. He had fallen asleep at his desk, with Lareina's cryptic message still unsolved.

"Yeah?" He answered wearily.

"Marc?"

"Yeah."

"It's Karl. We have a possible lead. It turns out that Dominick Covelli is Tony's brother. He's currently out on parole from those child molestation charges. He lives up in Fresno, though. We do have a number and an address."

"Oh wow! That's great Karl! Give me the info."

"Ok, his address is 355 Harmon Avenue." Karl shuffled through some papers before also giving Marc the phone number.

"Perfect. Let me call. If I get a hold of him, I'm driving back up there today, Karl."

"Yeah, I know, Marc. I knew you'd want to jump on this. Just let me know what happens."

"I will, Chief. Thanks."

Marc called Dominick's phone from his cell so as not to let on that the police were calling.

"Yo, this is Nick."

"Dominick Covelli?"

"Who wants to know?"

"My name is Detective Raymer."

"Oh Shit! Damn it, I knew I shouldn't have picked up!"

"Stop, Dominick. Now, listen. This isn't about you; it's about your brother."

"My brother? Tony?! What the hell is going on with Tony?"

"He's involved in a kidnapping. I need to speak to you."

"Fuck. Goddamn that kid!" Dominick's voice faltered.

"Listen to me carefully, Dominick. Very carefully. I'm coming up from Los Angeles. It's going to take me at least four to five hours to get there. Do you still live at 355 Harmon?"

"Yeah."

"Dominick, I want you in that house waiting for me. Do you understand? If you are not there by the time I reach Fresno, I will have your parole reversed in a heartbeat."

"I'll be here, Detective. I promise."

"You had better be."

"I will. I promise, I'll be waiting."

Marc hung up and called the Fresno police. He set up for two patrol cars to escort him to Dominick's house and ensure his safety.

"Ok, so what exactly did my brother get himself into?" Dominick asked nervously.

"That's what we want to know," Marc said sternly.

Dominick was a rather short, pudgy Italian male. His dark hair was slicked back. His eyes were dark, cold and shallow. He was fairly clean cut, though he did fashion a thick mustache on his upper lip. He even smoked a cigar as they talked. If Marc didn't know any better, he would have thought he was in a scene from The Sopranos just by looking at this man.

"Dominick, did you know your brother was a student at UCLA?"

"My brother's a fucking permanent student, Detective. He always just takes classes, but doesn't actually do anything with 'em."

"Ok," Marc said making notes from Dominick's answer. "When was the last time you spoke to your brother?"

"Oh shit, I don't know. Uhhhh...maybe like three months ago."

"Three months ago?! Are you kidding me? You mean to tell me that it's really been three months since you spoke to your own brother? Don't give me any bullshit, Dominick."

"I'm not, I swear. Tony and I don't have the best of relationships, if you know what I mean."

"Ok," Marc said cynically, "moving on. Do you know anything about a woman named Lareina Oliveira? Did Tony ever mention that name to you in the past?"

"Uhhhh...no. Who's that?"

"That's the woman your brother abducted."

"So, you weren't kidding on the phone."

"Do you think I'd drive all the way up here for a joke, Dominick?! Jesus, get real.

"Look, we need to know where he might have taken her. We have reason to believe they're somewhere up here, or possibly even somewhere east of here. Dominick, are there any places you can think of that he'd take her to?"

"No, Detective. I mean, we're from here originally. Tony moved to Los Angeles five years ago, but he grew up here. He knows the entire area inside and out. Our whole family does."

"Well, if this is where you're all from, are there any particular places that are special to the family in any way?"

Dominick looked down at the floor. "No, not that I can think of."

85

"Don't lie to me, Dominick! What about places where you grew up? Places you spent family vacations? The old family home? Anything?"

Hesitantly, Dominick replied, "no, nothing. Not a damn thing, Detective.

"My mom still lives in the same house from when we were kids. Tony hates her. He definitely wouldn't go there.

"And, uhhh...we didn't go on any family vacations or anything." Dominick was fishing for his words. Marc was having great difficulty believing this man.

"Oh, come on Dominick! You mean to tell me you never went camping in Yosemite or anything like that when you lived right here?!"

"Nope."

"He had to have taken her somewhere, Dominick! And I need to know where. I think you know exactly where they are."

"I don't know, Detective. I swear."

"Fine. Look, if you see him, his car, anything; if you hear anything, I want you to call me right away," Marc said as he handed Dominick his card.

"I will, Detective."

Marc left Fresno feeling extremely frustrated. Yet another day had passed, and the one possible lead they had ended up to be a complete flop. Marc instinctively knew that Dominick had lied to him, but he had no way to prove it. Not yet, anyway.

As he drove back to Los Angeles, Marc realized that he also hadn't heard back from Dr. Bauer.

Marc greatly feared that he would not be able to get to Lareina in time. He drove home as the sun was setting on another day on Lareina's kidnapping.

Chapter 10

Lareina lay on the blanket and Tony's rotund body was next to her, snoring. One whole day had passed since she sent that text message with her coordinates, yet she hadn't heard anything from Sandy, the police or even her family. She was beginning to give up all hope.

Tony began to stir. Slowly, he woke up.

"Ummm, Tony?"

"What?" He asked groggily.

"May I go outside to go to the bathroom?"

"Yeah, I don't see why not."

"Thank you," Lareina said meekly.

As Lareina walked out of the cabin, she saw their shoes on the porch. It was one of Tony's rules: no shoes inside the house.

She had worn kitten heels the day he abducted her. They weren't much, but perhaps she could use them to help lead people to save her. Maybe they could make a mark in a tree. The tree! That large tree she had noticed the other day would be an ideal landmark. This was the perfect opportunity. Quietly, she grabbed one of her shoes, and ran up to the large tree.

She reached as high as her short arm would allow, and began chipping away at the bark of the tree with her shoe. She hacked at it with all her might. Eventually, she began to notice that she was actually leaving a mark. This was going to take a while, though. Lareina decided that she would chip away at this tree's bark at every opportunity she had. It was a promise she made to herself; hoping that it would some how get her rescued.

Lareina knew that if she stayed out here any longer Tony would begin to become suspicious. She walked back to the cabin, placed the shoe exactly back the way it was, and walked back inside to whatever torturous plan Tony had in store for her today.

"Detective Raymer," Marc answered his cell phone.

"Detective, it's Dr. Bauer. I am so sorry I didn't call sooner. I didn't get your message until now. I've been out of town giving a lecture at a convention."

"That's fine," Marc dismissed Dr. Bauer's excuse. "Look, I need your expert opinion on this message as soon as possible. Can you come down to the station today so I can show it to you?"

"Yes, absolutely! I'll leave right away. I should be there in about thirty minutes."

It seemed like an eternity before Dr. Bauer finally arrived at the station. There was an anxious speed to her pace as she hastily walked over to Marc.

"Ok, let me see it. What is it? What does it say?"

Marc sat her down and showed her the message. "What does this mean, Dr. Bauer?"

Dr. Bauer looked at the message for a few moments. "Hmmm...it almost looks like trig."

"Trig?"

"Trigonometry, Detective. Let's see what we've got here.

"If you have a value for x and one for y, it's probably for some kind of graph as if they are coordinates of some sort."

Marc looked at the message, trying to imagine why Lareina would send them a message about a graph.

"You see, Detective, there's an x-axis and a y-axis. The x-axis is the vertical axis, and the y-axis is the horizontal axis."

Marc looked at the doctor, dumbfounded.

"Ok, the x-axis runs north to south. The y-axis runs east to west. Now, does that make sense?"

"Yes, that's more like my lingo."

"Ok. So we have a value on the x-axis equaling thirty degrees and forty four minutes. There's a value on the y-axis that equals one hundred nineteen degrees and approximately forty minutes."

"I'm not quite sure I understand, Doctor. How do you know that?"

"Look at her numbers, Detective Raymer. There's a small circle after the thirty seven. Just like you would put that small circle for degrees in temperature, that small circle equals degrees in latitude and longitude.

"The little line after the forty four equals minutes. That's another geographic marking."

"What does that little squiggly line mean?" Marc asked, pointing to the unusual looking line Lareina had put before the forty minutes listed in the y coordinates.

"That's an approximation. It means that it's not exactly forty minutes. It could be forty one minutes, it could be thirty nine. It could even be closer to...say forty five minutes."

"Well shit! What the hell do we do with an approximation like that?"

"I know it's tough and confusing, Detective. I understand. But this helps to narrow things down to a general area.

"I have to tell you that in my professional opinion, I think these are her geographic coordinates, Detective. I truly think she's trying to give us her location."

"You think these are her latitudinal and longitudinal coordinates?"

"Yes, I do, Detective. Whole heartedly. Detective Raymer, Lareina is extremely sharp. She figured these coordinates out somehow and sent them to us so we could find her."

"I don't doubt you, Dr. Bauer. But, is there any possibility that these numbers and symbols could stand for something else?"

"Well, I suppose that there is a slim possibility that they could stand for anything. But, knowing Lareina as I do; and with her giving us such specific x and y coordinates - she's giving us an exact point. If it's not her location, something important is definitely there."

"Are you sure?"

"Detective, you're asking me to be one hundred per cent sure about something that I can't be. But my intuition is telling me that's what this is. I'm ninety nine per cent sure."

"Well, one per cent doubt is the best shot we've had so far. I pray that you're right, Dr. Bauer."

"Listen Detective, Lareina is amazingly intelligent and resourceful. She was one of my smartest students ever. I have complete faith in her, and her ability to help us help her."

"Ok. I trust you and your intuition, Dr. Bauer.

"Thank you so much for your time and assistance."

"No problem, Detective. I'm more than happy to help!

"Please keep me updated."

"I most certainly will. Thank you again, Dr. Bauer."

Dr. Bauer then rose and walked away. Marc noticed her hands were clenched into fists as she walked. She had a visible nervousness to her.

Marc immediately called up to Brian.

"Brian?"

"Yeah, Marc. What is it?"

"I need you to tell me exactly where north thirty seven degrees forty four minutes and west one hundred nineteen degrees and approximately forty minutes is. I need that information ASAP."

"I'll get right on that, Marc. Call you back in a few."

"Great, thanks."

As soon as they hung up, Marc called Karl.

"Karl?"

"Yes. What is it Marcus?"

"Karl, we might have Lareina's location. I'm waiting for Brian to get back to me with the exact information. I want as many canine units as I can get, and we're all going to drive up there as soon as possible."

Marc heard Karl sigh.

"That's asking for a lot, Marc. But if you're sure we can save this girl today, then let's do it.

"Call me as soon as Brian gives you the exact data, and we'll send everyone out. I'll also call any and all local police stations once we know."

"Thanks, Chief. Call you back in a few."

Marc hung up. His heart started to race. Was it possible they'd finally save Lareina? They hadn't had such a solid lead in the case yet. He hoped that Dr. Bauer was right; that they could find Lareina's exact location. The one approximate coordinate still caused Marc to doubt everything, though.

Marc's car was one in a large caravan headed up north towards the mysterious coordinates. Local police were scheduled to meet them there. Local equine and canine officers had been dispatched as well.

"Hang in there, Lareina," Marc kept quietly saying to himself in the car. She was obviously very smart. All he could do was hope that she still had her wits about her, and that she was fighting for her life until he could come and rescue her.

The day had been passing along without incident. Lareina was amazed that Tony hadn't attempted to hurt her again.

They had eaten breakfast in silence. Tony insisted they played another card game, so they played war for a while.

Lunch time was approaching, and Tony decided to cook up some hot dogs again. Although thoroughly disgusted by her new diet, Lareina ate, knowing that her body desperately needed whatever nutrition she could get.

Since Tony was going to be preoccupied for at least a few minutes, Lareina decided this was another opportunity to carve on her tree.

"Tony, may I be excused to go to the bathroom while you cook?"

"Absolutely, my dear." He kissed her on the cheek.

Feeling sick to her stomach because of Tony's kiss, Lareina stepped out. She noticed that the one shoe's heel was clearly more worn than the other. This time she grabbed both shoes. Tony was extremely detail oriented. Lareina knew that he would absolutely notice if one heel was more worn than the other. She dared not risk letting him figure out her plan.

She ran up to the tree, and again began carving into it as hard as she could. She created an "x" on the tree, hoping that would be enough of a signal that she was there. She dug as hard as she could with both shoes. Only now was the bark truly indented.

Knowing she had little time left, she stopped carving. She quickly turned on her phone. No messages. "Damn," she whispered to herself. She hoped that her message with her coordinates had reached Sandy.

The phone quietly beeped at her, indicating the battery was starting to run low. She quickly turned it off, and placed it back into her pocket. She grabbed her shoes and ran back to the cabin. She carefully placed the shoes back exactly where they were. She opened the door to the cabin, and walked in.

Just as she entered the main room of the cabin, she was suddenly jerked back. Tony had grabbed her thick hair, and pulled her towards him. Once again, he held the knife to her neck.

"Where were you?" He grunted.

"I was going to the bathroom."

"Really? I find that rather hard to believe. What took you so damn long?"

"I – I'm sorry, Tony. It...uhhh...took longer than I expected. I didn't realize I had to go that much. It wasn't planned, I promise.

"I'm sorry. I'm really very sorry, Tony. It was completely out of my control. Please forgive me," Lareina begged and pleaded hoping that it would be enough to spare her.

"I guess I can let that slide...this time." He pushed her forward.

She landed on her hands and knees. Her already beaten and abused body now acquired even more scrapes, cuts, and bruises.

"Time for lunch," Tony sneered, and walked into the kitchen.

Lareina took a deep breath, and slowly stood up. As much as she hated the idea, she knew she had to walk into the kitchen to have lunch with her vicious and unpredictable captor.

Marc, along with the countless other Los Angeles and local police officers were searching everywhere. They walked through endless trees and brush. They searched all around the river. Not one stone had been left unturned.

Dogs were sniffing for miles. There were a few times the canines indicated they had picked up her scent, but then the trails eventually faded away. The dogs were unable to pick up her smell again.

People were looking all over for any sign of Lareina. Every little detail was considered: foot tracks, excrement, clothing, possibly even her dead body. If the ground looked odd or out of sorts in any way, officers would begin digging, seeing if her body had been buried. Much to their dismay - and elation - her body was never found.

The mounted officers rode through the river, going in every direction, searching for a few miles, but were unable to find any possible signs of life, or any clues.

Fliers with Lareina's information, and all the other pertinent information regarding her kidnapping were nailed into innumerable trees within the area, in the hopes that a passing hiker or camper might see them.

After endless hours of searching, an exhausted and extremely frustrated Marc walked back to his car and called Karl. He decided to sit in the car with the doors shut; something told him he'd need privacy for this conversation.

"Karl?"

"Yes, Marc."

"We haven't found anything. No clues, no body, no signs of human life here at all."

Karl was silent for a moment, and then sighed heavily. "Call it off, Marcus."

"What?"

"You heard me. Call it off.

"Obviously, if that many officers can't find a damn thing, he's moved on and cleared his tracks well."

"I thought we had this one, Karl. I really did.

"Maybe if we expand the search we can find tire tracks, or something."

"I know this is tough, Marcus. But it has to be done. We could expand the search to the entire state of California, but it's just not feasible. We cannot afford this kind of money and man power. Not without more significant evidence."

"But according to Brian, this was it. The exact location. The location that she gave us! We're south of Elephant rock, over by Yosemite and the Merced River. I just don't get it, Karl. There's absolutely nothing here but trees.

"Brian had the exact location. I don't understand how we could have missed them."

"I'm sorry, Marcus. I really am. You know I want to find her as much as you do. But, we're gonna have to call this one off until we can get a better lead."

"Damn it!" Marc yelled, and hit his hand against the steering wheel of his car.

"I know it sucks, but you have to do it Marc."

"Yes, Chief," Marc's voice was weak and crushed. He hated to give up. They were so close to rescuing Lareina, but yet somehow they had missed her. Marc did not want to abandon the search, but he knew he had no choice.

Marc hung up, got out of his car and reluctantly gathered the officers around him to tell them the bad news.

He thanked everyone for their hard work and assistance. He explained that Karl was officially calling off the search for today. Marc told them he hoped they would band together again, and find her very soon.

The group dispersed.

Everyone loaded their tools, equipment, and belongings into their various vehicles.

Marc loaded up quickly, and drove back to Los Angeles before anyone else. His disappointment and frustration had gotten the better of him, and he did not want to stay in that forest one minute longer than was necessary.

Marc lay in his bed, his hands resting behind his head. He couldn't sleep at all. Thoughts were racing through his mind.

Something was wrong. Terribly wrong.

Lareina was smart. Far too smart to make such a huge error. She wouldn't have made a mistake and sent them looking in the wrong direction. This was a legitimate kidnapping. She was trying to help them, not prolong her suffering.

Marc went over every detail - even the tiniest of details, from the entire day in his head. They went by the exact coordinates Brian had given him. Brian was extremely thorough and detailed. It would be odd to even consider that a mistake had been made on his part, though Marc knew anything was possible at this point.

Marc could not comprehend the fact that they hadn't found anything at all. No foot prints, no clothes. They hadn't even found tire marks indicating the Mustang had ever been there. They had to have been searching in the wrong area.

How could that have happened? How could they have been lead astray? Where had the mistake been made?

They were losing valuable time. Lareina's life still remained in grave danger. They were spending hours on end, and a tremendous amount of man power all on nothing!

Had she been wrong in her coordinates? Lareina seemed far too detail oriented for that to have happened. But, perhaps she was only assuming her locale. Where and how had she gotten those coordinates? Did she use her phone's GPS, or some unusual mathematical way of determining where she might be? Who knew? There was no way to answer that; to know how she came up with those numbers and coordinates. It seemed odd to Marc that she would just guess. Somehow she must have logically come to those numbers. All Marc could do was hope it was through a reliable method.

Yet somehow, someway, a mistake had been made – a terrible mistake. Lareina still was nowhere to be found because of it.

"Damn it!" Marc screamed out into his empty apartment. His scream echoed loudly.

He had to find her, and soon. He could not let time continue to tick away while she was being held hostage by some insane man. He shuddered to think at what Tony might be doing to her.

He continued to lay in bed; the day's events playing on an endless loop in his mind. Marc knew he would not sleep at all tonight.

Chapter 11

Lareina knew she couldn't take another chance of aggravating Tony. It was night, and he was dead asleep. Quickly and quietly, she exited the cabin. She grabbed her shoes and ran up to her tree.

By the dim light of the slight crescent moon above, she could see what she had done so far, and how much more she needed to do in order to make a significant mark on this enormous tree.

Lareina instantly mustered up all the energy she could and began chipping away at the tree's bark once again. She scraped and she hacked at it with all her might. Using both shoes this time, Lareina repeatedly carved her "x" pattern into the giant tree.

Lareina worked ceaselessly in her carving of the tree. She made her "x" as large and as deep as she could. As Lareina continuously carved her "x" into the tree, she hoped that it would was enormous enough to grab someone's attention. Minutes and hours flew by along with the chips of tree bark. Lareina continually carved into her sacred tree all night.

Finally, Lareina could see that dawn was beginning to break. She'd need to return to the cabin soon so Tony wouldn't suspect anything.

She looked at her "x." It was carved fairly deeply into the bark of the tree. Its expanse was nearly the entire width of the tree, and its height seemed to be large enough that no one could miss it. Lareina was proud of herself: she had done well. She had hacked so much into the tree that the heels on her shoes were worn to mere nubs.

Satisfied with her work, Lareina ran back to the cabin. She quietly placed her shoes back, and went inside the cabin.

Tony was still sleeping. Lareina carefully slid onto the blanket, so as not to disturb him. She rolled over and closed her eyes, hoping to get just a tiny bit of rest before this new day actually began.

Lareina sat on her knees and gazed out the window, watching the late morning sunlight dance through the trees. She wondered if anyone was out trying to save her. It certainly didn't seem that way. Perhaps she was fated to this existence with Tony, and to whatever the outcome of this situation might be.

Tony reentered the cabin after having relieved himself. "I want to dance."

Lareina turned around and looked at him confusedly. "What?"

"Stand up. I said that I want to dance."

Reluctantly, she rose and walked over to Tony. She awkwardly placed her hands on his shoulders. He had no problem resting his hands on her round hips. She closed her eyes and tried to think of something else so as to distract herself from the uneasy feeling she experienced from his touch.

The two began to slowly circle in the cabin. The only music was the old wooden floor creaking under the weight of their feet. They circled and circled and circled the entire main room of the cabin countless times.

Tony wore a grin that was akin to that of a child at a carnival. This was better than he had ever dreamed.

After what could have been either minutes or even hours of their slow circling dance Tony said, "now I want to learn how to cha-cha."

Lareina stopped and looked at him in complete surprise. "What?"

"I want to learn how to cha-cha. You're Hispanic; you know how to do it. So, teach me!"

Lareina was dumbstruck. "Are you kidding me?"

"No! Teach me how to cha-cha, God damn it!" Tony screamed like a child throwing a temper tantrum.

"Ok, ok." Lareina sighed.

She positioned him so that he was standing next to her. "Ok, so the rhythm is one-two-cha-cha-cha. Got it?

"The first thing you want to do is stick your foot out." Lareina demonstrated. Her hips swiveled in a way that Tony could not ignore, or resist.

Tony then put his fat, clumsy foot forward just as Lareina had instructed.

"Good. Now, swing it out as you step back, and then take three quick little steps. Like this." Lareina's Latin dancing ability was enchanting to Tony.

Tony attempted to follow Lareina's lead but his chubby, heavy feet clunked on the floor.

Lareina paused, thinking of a way to get Tony to be lighter on his feet. "Do you know what the ball of your foot is?" Lareina asked.

"Yeah. Why?"

"You see, in Latin dancing, we're often on the balls of our feet. It's light. That's why Latin dancers move so fluidly.

"Try that again, but do it on the balls of your feet."

Tony tried Lareina's suggestion. There was a slight improvement.

"There, that's better. You're getting it," she tried to encourage him. She figured positive interaction would keep her alive, at least for now.

"I was sure you'd be a good dancer, but how do you know so much about this?" Tony asked.

"I don't know. At parties, family gatherings and special occasions, everyone in my family would salsa, merengue or cha-cha. We were always dancing. I guess it's just second nature.

"When I was a child, I used to watch the professional dancers on the television. The women were so beautiful to watch. Their movements were so fluid and gorgeous. I wanted to be like them, to be able to move like that.

"So, I studied their every movement. I watched how their bodies would twist and turn. I would practice mimicking them in my room, in front of my mirror for hours."

"My little dancer."

"Me, a dancer? No," Lareina scoffed. "A wannabe, maybe – at best."

Tony sat down. Lareina awkwardly followed suit.

"What made you choose algebra?" He quietly asked her.

Lareina was taken aback. Who was this man sitting in front of her? What had stirred inside of him to want to dance, and now get to know her as person? He suddenly appeared gentile and genuine. Lareina simply could not understand what went on in this man's mind.

Was it possible that Tony wasn't an entirely bad man after all? Maybe he was just terribly misunderstood. Maybe the problem wasn't in his behavior, but in everyone's reactions towards him. Perhaps his anger was simply misdirected. He just seemed so harmless now. Lareina could not make sense of it at all. Tony's actions were extremely perplexing.

"Well, I learned early on that I was good at math," she explained. "When we studied algebra in high school and I figured out my first equation properly, I felt like I had accomplished something. I was very proud of myself; it meant so much to me. I've also always found algebra to be very easy.

"As I got older, I purposefully took harder and harder classes in algebra. They challenged me, but the math still came to me rather easily. Like dancing, it was second nature, I guess.

"Anyway, I just loved it so much, and I thought I wanted to share that same passion for math with the students of Los Angeles. I have been teaching math at a local high school for years now."

"Which one?"

"Oh, it doesn't matter, Tony. They're all the same."

Tony glared at her for a moment, unsatisfied with her answer. He wanted to know where she taught; after a few moments of silence, he decided to let it go.

"Anyway, I taught my students well and tried desperately to share my passion with them.

"Some students - even learning disabled students, just shined like stars. They surprised me and did incredibly well. That was more than rewarding. Those experiences were definitely worth it.

"The majority, however, did not do well. No matter what I did, no matter what methods or tricks I used, they just hated the subject."

"Maybe you weren't teaching them correctly."

"No, it wasn't that. They understood, I know they did. They simply did not care. They wouldn't do their homework; they wouldn't put any effort into the class. It bored them, I guess. Some of my fellow teachers had similar issues with the same students. There was such apathy and lack of ambition. We all did whatever we could to teach those kids, but nothing ever seemed to work.

"Whatever it was, their hearts just weren't into math the way mine is.

"It was a very bad situation for me. You see, I need to be surrounded by people who are as passionate as I am. I need to be in a positive environment. I simply was not getting it from teaching those high school kids.

"So, I decided to go get my Ph. D. so that I could teach at the university level. I want to teach math majors and students who truly care.

"What about you, Tony?"

"I don't know.

"My brain needs to be constantly occupied. I've studied everything: languages, history, philosophy, science, and math. Nothing fulfilled me. Nothing was ever challenging enough.

"I took this class as just another class to take.

"I don't know what I want to do. I need to find something that stimulates me on an intellectual level. I still haven't found it yet, though.

"How old are you, Lareina?"

"Thirty two. Why? How old are you?

"Thirty eight, believe it or not. I'm pushing forty and I still have no direction or calling in life. I'm a permanent student, as my brother calls me."

"That's not necessarily a bad thing, Tony.

"You're clearly a very intelligent man. You just need to find something that fits you, so to speak."

"Yeah, I guess you're right."

Tony leaned forward and planted a big, wet, cold, sloppy kiss on Lareina's lips. She cringed as he kissed her. She refused to even consider kissing him back; she was absolutely sickened by this kiss. Though he seemed very gentle and even harmless at the moment, she was still greatly disgusted by this strange, fat man.

Having pulled away from her captor and his sloppy kiss, Lareina sat next to Tony, and gazed out the window, quietly wondering what was going to happen next in this strange saga.

The rest of the afternoon had passed quietly when Lareina excused herself and went out to a tree. The sun was just beginning to set on yet another day in her captivity.

Still not knowing if her messages were reaching Sandy, she tried one last text message. It was all her battery could handle.

"X marks the spot. Large tree – walking path. Merced River, north of Ele-"

She was cut off; Tony had come up behind her. He grabbed her shoulder.

Quickly, she pressed the send button, and the phone declared her message had been sent.

"Your cell phone?!" He screamed at her. "You little fucking bitch! You've had that all this time and have been using it to reach other people?"

"No, no. Tony, I...uhhh..."

"Don't lie to me!

"I can't fucking believe this! I trusted you! I fucking trusted you! I gave you the privilege of coming out here, unbound. And this is how you fucking thank me?! God damn it!"

Tony grabbed the phone from Lareina's tiny little hand and launched it into the air. The small device flew quite far, and eventually it sank into the river.

Tony grabbed Lareina's arm, dragged her out from around the tree and threw her to the ground.

Lareina sat motionless for a moment. Tony came up behind her, and grabbed her by her hair, and turned her to face him.

"You fucking bitch!" He screamed right in her face. His spit landed on her.

He threw her backwards by her hair. Lareina fell on her back into a pile of dirt, pebbles, and leaves.

Tony came running up to her. Lareina reacted quickly and kicked Tony in the crotch. He fell to his knees.

Lareina jumped up and began running around the forest, screaming for help at the top of her lungs. "Help! Someone, please help me!" She ran a few more steps. "Help! Help me, please!" There was no answer, but yet she continued to scream as she ran, in the hopes that someone would find her.

Lareina ran in the direction away from her sacred, carved tree in the hopes that Tony would never see what else she had done. She feared what he might do should he ever see the mark on the tree.

Lareina ran as fast she could. The forest was endless, but she felt that as long as she ran away from the cabin, she had to be headed in the right direction.

Tony eventually caught up with her. From behind, he pushed Lareina forward to the ground. She fell with a loud thud. He then stepped on her back, and began increasing the amount of weight and pressure he put on her.

"I told you that if I couldn't have you, nobody else could. Is that what you want?"

Unable to breathe because of the pressure on her back, all Lareina could do was grunt.

"Well, is it?"

"No," her voice was extremely weak as vital air escaped her lungs when she spoke.

"I didn't think so." He finally removed his foot from her back.

Lareina began taking in deep breaths of air while still laying down.

"This should keep you occupied while I get the tape," Tony said as he slashed her leg through her pants, and created yet another deep wound on her beautiful body.

Lareina cried out in pain. Slowly, she sat up and looked at the injury he had just inflicted upon her. It was a large, deep, nasty wound on her calf.

Unlike her arm, she wasn't being given gauze to clean it. She quickly ripped off the remainder of her pant leg. She tried to dab the large slice, but it was bleeding very heavily. She ripped off a piece of the fabric and made a tourniquet. She tied it on her leg just above the wound, to help slow down the bleeding until she could tend to the wound properly.

While Tony was still gone, Lareina gingerly pulled herself up and began limping away as fast as she could. She knew not to call out this time as Tony would follow her voice.

She ran as fast as she could. It was difficult for her to make her way through the forest. She eventually found a very large tree and hid behind it. As she sat, she noticed just how badly her leg was bleeding. Large drops of blood cascaded off her leg onto the leaves under her.

"You little fucking bitch! Where the hell are you?" Tony screamed out. His voice echoed throughout the woods.

Lareina held her breath so as not to make a sound to lead him to her.

The rest of the forest remained silent.

"God damn you, Lareina! I am going to find you!"

Lareina sat as still as possible. She took in tiny, quiet breaths so Tony wouldn't even notice her breathing.

Her leg was still bleeding heavily. Lareina knew she had to do something.

Slowly and quietly, she ripped off another piece of material from her other pant leg. She took the new piece and placed it directly over the wound. She then untied the tourniquet, placed it over the other piece of material and tied it so that there was pressure being applied right onto the wound. It wasn't a spectacular bandage, but it would have to do for now.

"Where are you? You have to be around here somewhere, you bitch!" Tony cried out. She could hear that he was getting closer. Lareina knew that she needed to run, but she didn't want him to see her. She prayed there was a way for her to get closer to safety without Tony ever noticing her movements.

Lareina peered around the tree. Thankfully, Tony's back was to her, and he was a little ways away from her. She carefully got up and hobbled further away as quickly as possible.

There was a small tree just ahead. Lareina limped behind it and laid down, so Tony wouldn't see her.

The sunlight had dwindled down to almost nothing. Lareina stayed behind her tree, waiting for night to fall. She decided that she would run to freedom under the black blanket of the night. The ground under the tree was a cold, hard home for her, but it would have to suffice until she could move again.

"Fuck!" Tony's voice could be heard echoing. "God damn it, Lareina! You will come back to me! You can't escape from me! You're mine, and you will always be with me! I'll find you!"

Lareina lay still behind her little tree for a couple of hours. Once the night sky fully hid her, Lareina slowly got up, and began to walk away. She tried to move quietly in case Tony was still out in the woods hunting her. She hobbled in the direction of the walking path that passed by her carved tree. The tree was about a mile back from where she was now which meant the path was over a mile away north of her. Slowly, she continued to make her way further and further away from the horrid cabin.

As the night progressed, the shadows of the forest became quite confusing. Lareina was beginning to lose her sense of direction. All of the trees began to look alike. She could no longer tell where she had come from and the direction in which she was trying to go.

Lareina decided that any movement was better than nothing. She continued to limp aimlessly through the woods in the hopes that she would find the path or a person.

She walked for hours. Her body was becoming extremely tired and weak as the night progressed. She knew she needed to rest, but she feared being re-captured by Tony.

Finally physically unable to go any further, Lareina hid behind a large tree. She sat up and closed her eyes, hoping to get some rest for her weary body.

The sunrise came too soon for Lareina. As dawn began to break, she knew she needed to continue on her path to freedom. The morning light was helping her to see the forest more clearly.

Painfully, Lareina rose and began limping towards the walking path. It appeared tiny from where she stood, but it was within her view. That view motivated Lareina to keep going despite the great pain in her leg. Lareina knew it would take her a while to get to the path, but that was her path to safety and she wasn't going to stop now. She was too close: she could taste her freedom.

The day continued on as Lareina inched her way towards the path.

It was about high noon when she finally made it onto the walking path. Lareina felt great relief and excitement. She was going to be rescued soon! One solitary joyful tear escaped her hazel eyes. She began walking on the path, knowing that another person just had to be on this same path: someone who could help her.

As the afternoon wore on Lareina's pace had slowed down significantly, but she continued to limp on the walking path. Her determination was far too great for her to simply give up.

In the distance, she thought she heard a car. Was it possible that she was closer to being rescued than she thought?

With hopes of being rescued, Lareina tried to limp just a little faster. The sound of the car was coming closer and closer, until she realized the car was actually coming from behind her. She turned around just in time to see that it was Tony's Mustang. Lareina froze with fear as the car approached. Tony didn't stop, and he pushed Lareina down with the force of his car. Lareina dropped to the ground instantly.

Tony got out of the car. Lareina lay on the ground unable to move from pain, and in complete shock that he had found her. Her heart broke as she realized that her hopes for freedom were being taken away from her.

"Did you really think you could get away from me?"

Lareina was unable to respond.

"Well?!"

Again, she was silent.

"I already told you, you belong to me. You cannot get away. If I can't have you, no one can!" Tony pulled Lareina up by her arm. He already had the electrical tape in his hand.

He tightly taped her ankles together.

In seeing how she had tended to her new injury, Tony ripped off a large piece of tape."Take that off!" He ordered, indicating towards her home made bandage and tourniquet.

Unwillingly, Lareina untied her tourniquet, took the pieces of fabric off her leg, and shoved them into her pants pocket. The bleeding had stopped, but the wound looked raw. Tony harshly slapped the large piece of electrical tape over her wound.

Tony grabbed both of Lareina's arms and pulled them over her head before he began taping them tightly.

He pulled her up, and dragged her behind him into the car.

Lareina looked out the window at the endless trees as they drove back. She had come so close to freedom, and yet it had been stolen from her in the blink of an eye. They drove for a few miles in agonizing silence.

Tony parked a small distance away from the cabin. He got out of the car, came around and pulled Lareina out. He dragged her by her arms all the way back to the cabin. Her body was pounded and dirtied by the leaves and rocks on the ground.

Once inside he threw her on to the cold, hard, splintery, wooden floor. She rolled a few times due to his force. All she could feel was pain shooting throughout her body.

"Remember that music I played in the car?"

"Yes," Lareina huffed as she struggled for air, and a reprieve from all the pain.

"That's a German heavy metal band.

"In one of their older Cd's, they have a song called, Klavier.

"Klavier is German for piano.

"The story behind the song is that a man hears a pianist playing, and he falls in love with her music.

"She is so talented, that he actually becomes obsessed with her playing.

"He kidnaps her, and brings her to his home. There, he chains her to the piano and forces her to play day and night. He doesn't feed or care for her.

"She eventually dies from starvation and dehydration, still chained to the piano.

"In the end of the song the man admits the irony of his obsession actually killing and ending the one thing he ever truly loved.

"Perhaps I need to do something similar with you. Maybe that will get you to understand."

Lareina was appalled at the story Tony just told her. Could he really be serious? What kind of sick person thinks like that? Confused and scared, Lareina pleaded with him, "no, no. Tony, please..."

"Do you play the piano, or any other instruments?"

"No," one lone tear ran down her cheek. Lareina quickly wiped it away with her arm; she didn't want Tony to think she was weak or vulnerable.

"I should get a desk, chain you to that, and make you do algebraic equations all day.

"That would work." Tony chuckled at his own idea. "Ya know what? I actually kind of like that idea.

"Let's sleep on that one, shall we?" Tony then sat in the rocking chair, intensely watching Lareina's every movement.

The sun was gone now, and just a tiny glimmer of light from the moon came in through the old, faded windows.

Lareina hoped and prayed with all of her might that Tony would forget his devious plan. For now, she could only lie down on the floor, bound and beaten, and wait for what tomorrow would bring.

Chapter 12

Marc sat at his desk, staring once again at Lareina's coded message that had sent police from across the state of California on a wild goose chase. What on Earth did all of this mean? Dr. Bauer seemed so sure that the message gave Lareina's geographical coordinates, yet they were unsuccessful in finding her. Marc wondered if the numbers and symbols could possibly represent anything else. If so, what? Dr. Bauer hadn't indicated any other solid possibilities. His mind was completely baffled.

Marc was startled back into reality from a call on his desk phone.

"Yeah?"

"Marcus?"

"Yes, Karl?"

"What are you doing?"

"Trying to decipher Lareina's message. Somehow a mistake was made, and I have to figure it out so we can find her."

"Marcus, I'm going to need you to put that one down for now.

"We just got a call about another missing person."

"Adult or child?"

"Teenager. And I need you to head up that case."

"No," Marc said without even thinking. He refused to give up on Lareina and he didn't care if it angered his boss.

"Damn it, Marcus! She's been gone for a while – too long, if you ask me. For all we know she's dead, and we know for a fact that this one isn't! This boy just went missing this morning."

"Karl, for all we know Lareina is still alive, waiting for us to come and rescue her. That is our job, you know. Regardless of how much time has passed, we can't give up."

"Marcus, I need you on this one."

"No," he boldly repeated himself. After a pause, Marc said, "Come on, you could have Joseph or Tom head that one up. You don't need me for this case, Karl."

Karl was silent on the other end of the line.

"Alright, look, Karl. I'll be happy to do small follow up calls or what have you, but I am not heading up another case. Period. The Oliveira case is still my top priority. Got it?"

Karl could be heard sighing out of frustration on the other end. "Fine."

Karl hung up and Marc went back to studying his cryptic message.

Marc had been looking at the message for far too long. Several hours had passed, and Marc didn't even realize it! It was already well passed noon. "Shit," Marc thought to himself as he realized more time was ticking away, and they still weren't any closer to finding Lareina.

Marc decided to call up to Brian to check and see if the coordinates could have been reversed.

"Hello?" It was Oswald. Oswald worked up stairs with Brian. He had a deep, rich, velvety, sensuous voice similar to that of Isaac Hayes or Barry White. "He really should have gone into radio instead of becoming a cop," Marc thought to himself.

"Hey Oswald, it's Marcus."

"Hey Marc! What's up?"

"Has Brian given you any information on my Oliveira case?"

"Yeah, why?"

112

"Did he give you those geographical coordinates?"

"Yes he did, Marc."

"Oswald, is it possible that the coordinates were reversed?"

"Possible? No, not really. Well, it's not likely anyway. Not with numbers like that. Marc, if those numbers were backwards or reversed she'd be somewhere odd like the arctic or the middle of the ocean or something. I could look them up though, if you want. We could see exactly where they would point, but I have to tell you that I find it highly unlikely that it would be a legitimate locale."

"Damn it!"

"I know this case is really getting to you, Marc."

"I'm sorry I can't be of any more help."

"It's ok, Oswald. I greatly appreciate your help. It's just that a huge mistake was made somewhere, and I'm trying to figure it out. Thank you, though."

Marc hung up and buried his face in his hands. This was one of the most difficult and confusing cases he had ever worked on.

He sighed heavily, but knew he couldn't lose any more valuable time. "Back to it," he told himself. He stared deeply at the mysterious message once again.

Dawn was just beginning break when Tony woke up Lareina. "Honey, I've been thinking. The piano idea really is unique. But, I don't have a piano. Hell, I don't even have a table. But I do have the rocking chair. So I've decided that we're gonna use that."

Lareina looked up with him, with large doe-like eyes. The magnitude of her fear was easy to see.

Tony picked up the rocking chair and placed it next to Lareina. He took out his knife and cut her wrist bindings. Tony was paying little attention to what he was doing and he cut Lareina's wrist. Once again, blood began to ooze from her now very fragile body.

"It's a small cut, it should be ok. The bleeding should stop fairly quickly. It's just another new scar in the making. I'll be fine," Lareina said to herself, trying to remain strong and stoic.

Tony grabbed Lareina's wrists and taped them around a post in the leg of the rocking chair.

After he was finished, Tony stepped back and admired his handiwork. "Not bad at all," he chuckled. "We're definitely going to have to keep this going for a while."

Lareina inhaled deeply, fighting back tears. Carefully, she slid back so she was laying down and was as comfortable as possible. She closed her eyes, wishing that this would all be over when she awoke.

Lareina slowly opened her eyes, realizing that she was still laying in the same spot next to the rocking chair. She could tell by the glow in the window it was late afternoon.

The day had passed, and she hadn't moved at all. She hadn't eaten, either. Tony never offered her any food or water, but it didn't matter since she wasn't hungry anyway.

Lareina had given up all hope now. She only had that one chance to escape, and she failed. No one had come to her rescue; they hadn't even returned her messages. Lareina knew now that she would never be rescued. There was no way it was possible. It was too late now. She let the day slip away as she simply lay in defeat.

While the clock continued to tick away, and Marc stared at his copy of Lareina's message, an idea finally came to him.

He called Oswald again.

"Hello, Oswald. It's Marcus again."

"What can I do for ya, Marc?"

"Oswald, do you have those coordinates we gave you written somewhere - anywhere up there?"

"No, not right in front of me. I'd have to hunt them down, Marc. Brian's out today, so it might take me a little while – you know how his filing system is."

"Yeah, I do. If you even want to call it a filing system. Anyway that's fine, Oswald. Just call me as soon as you can."

"Will do, Marc."

"Thank you, Oswald. Much appreciated."

Tony was eating late again. This time he ate while sitting in the rocking chair. He was so proud of his creation that he just had to sit in the chair. He felt as if he was a part of living artwork sitting that chair with Lareina taped to its leg. What beauty and sheer genius! This old rocking chair was now a throne: his throne.

Tony continued to eat; his mind was stuck in his own little world. If a crumb fell and Tony wasn't looking, Lareina would try to eat it from the floor. She was struggling greatly with learning how to move and eat without her hands. Sometimes she succeeded in obtaining the food bits; sometimes they taunted her, sitting just out of reach.

A large piece of food fell in front of Lareina. She looked up at Tony. He was watching the night sky through the faded window. She knew she only had once chance at getting this food.

As covertly as she could, Lareina wiggled her way forward inch by inch. She continually checked to see if Tony was looking. His mind was still somewhere else, so she continued on her quest.

She was now within reach of the large crumb. She extended her neck forward, leaned her head to the side and reached for it with her mouth. As she turned and lowered her head a floorboard creaked, snapping Tony right back to reality.

He looked down at her struggling madly to get the piece of food. He kicked the food away. Then he stomped heavily on her arm with his large foot, laughing heartily. "No, no, my dear. You don't get any of that. You don't deserve to eat after what you did. I do have to say that it was a good effort, though."

Lareina lay on the floor with her face down, feeling completely thwarted. With a sigh, she closed her eyes and hoped that the new day would somehow bring her to safety.

It was a few minutes after eleven at night when Marc was finally driving home after such an exhausting and frustrating day.

While driving on the freeway, his cell phone rang.

"Detective Raymer."

"Detective, this is Sandy Taylor."

"Oh, hello, Miss Taylor. What can I do for you at this hour of the night?"

"Detective, I got another text from Lareina. It's another strange one. Would you mind coming over?"

"No, not at all," he sighed. "I'll be there shortly." Marc got off at the next exit and began to head in the other direction, towards Sandy's house.

In less than twenty minutes, Marc was back at Sandy and Lareina's home.

"So, let me see this text message," Marc said getting straight down to business. He was far too tired to make small talk with Sandy.

Sandy brought over her phone and showed him the latest message. "X marks the spot. Large tree; walking path. Merced River, north of Ele-"

"What does that mean, Detective?"

Marcus shook his head. "I don't know, Miss Taylor.

116

"And to be perfectly honest, I am far too worn out to even begin to try to decipher it right now. Let me copy it down and I'll look at it at the precinct tomorrow."

While Marc copied down Lareina's message, Sandy moved closer to him on the couch.

"Oh, you poor thing," Sandy's tone changed. Her voice was now quiet, soothing, and enticing. "You must be so tired from working so hard on this case. You're such a kind, selfless, giving person. You literally dedicate your life to helping others.

"I know there's so much stress in your job. You know, I can help you relax.

"We're both going through so much with Lareina being missing and all. I mean, it's such an emotional experience for us both." Sandy began gently and seductively caressing Marc's leg. "I think we both just need something to distract us from all of this." Her hand began working its way up toward his groin.

Trying to remain calm, Marc continued to look at the message and quietly said, "no thank you, Miss Taylor."

Sandy dismissed Marc's words and continued to try to tempt the handsome policeman. Her fingers delicately traveled up his leg. She leaned in closer to him, hoping that she might even be able to kiss him. She had become greatly infatuated with him since she first saw him. Marc was so handsome and well built. His British accent was irresistible. He was the kind of man she could only fantasize about, and now he was in her home, sitting next to her. Sandy simply could not contain herself any longer. Although she truly wanted to save Lareina, she also wanted Marc – badly.

Marc repeated himself. "No, Miss Taylor."

Sandy did not heed Marc's rejections. Instead, her hands continued to wander over his muscular body through his suit.

Marc finally shot up off the couch out of frustration. "Look, I have what I need here. Thank you for the message, Miss Taylor. I do appreciate it.

"But remember, this is strictly business. We're here for Lareina, and nothing more. We have to bring her home, and as soon as possible. That is our one and only focus right now."

Sandy slumped down into the couch, pouting.

Marc took his copy of Lareina's newest message, and quickly exited Sandy's home.

He got into his car and sighed.He was stunned by Sandy's behavior. He could not understand what would drive her to act that way when her best friend and roommate had been missing for so long. All he wanted to do was bring Lareina home safely, and he assumed she wanted the same. This case was becoming far too dramatic and chaotic for his liking. He hit the steering wheel out frustration.

Marc started his car and drove away from Sandy's place quickly. He eventually made his way home in the dark winter night.

Chapter 13

Lareina awoke to Tony rocking back and forth in the chair. She was being pulled forwards and backwards with the motion of the chair. She held her hands and her face up weakly, trying not to be crunched by the weight of the chair and Tony. Due to her starvation and dehydration from the past twenty four hours, she fought to keep herself up with the waves of the chair. Yet she found her hands and face slipping closer and closer to the ground.As she felt herself slipping closer to the ground, she would pull herself back up with all of her might. She battled her fatigue as best she could, but her body was too weak to for to hold herself up for too much longer.

Her hands finally fell to the ground and with just one push, all of Tony's fat weight and the weight of the chair crashed down on Lareina's delicate little hands. Tony purposefully rested there for a moment, crunching down on Lareina's hands. Lareina screamed out in pain.

Tony got out of the chair, and harshly slapped Lareina across the face. "Don't you ever scream like that again! Do I make myself clear?"

Lareina looked up at Tony through her tearful eyes and nodded. She slumped back down to the floor and tried to fight the pain that resided in her hands. They began to swell and bruise almost instantly. Lareina looked away, as if not seeing her newest injury would make it so that it never really happened.

As she lay on the floor, the piece of pant material she had ripped for her make-shift tourniquet peered out of the top of her pocket and caught her eye. Lareina knew that she needed to use that fabric. Somehow, someway, she was going to use that piece of material to help direct people to help save her.

Just as she began to think of various ways to the material, Tony surprised her and cut her hand ties, grabbed her by the ankles and dragged her into the kitchen. The floor scrapped, splintered and cut her body as they made their way into the kitchen.

Once they reached the kitchen, he re-taped her hands together. He sat her up and handed her a dish with some unrecognizable form of food on it and a fork. He forced her to eat with her hands still taped. They ate in a deafening silence.

As she ate the unremarkable food, Lareina tried to conjure up a way to get Tony out of the cabin for an extended period of time. It wouldn't be easy. She needed to have an excuse – a good excuse. One that he couldn't debate. Then the idea came to her.

While eating, Lareina scrunched down and began to moan in pain.

"What's wrong now?" Tony asked impatiently.

"Oh, it's nothing, Tony. It's – it's – I just got my time of the month, that's all."

"What?! You got your God damn period?!" Tony was clearly angry with her.

"Yes I did. I'm sorry, Tony," Lareina meekly replied.

"Yeah, well. You should be. You need to fucking control that shit, Lareina." He paused before he realized the full implications of this situation. "Damn it, you're gonna need stuff! I can't have you bleeding all over the place. Fuck!"

"I'm so sorry Tony. I didn't mean to cause any problems."

"Yeah, whatever. Now, I'm gonna have to drive into a town to get you supplies.

"Damn you, bitch!" Tony again slapped Lareina with great strength.

Lareina said nothing, she didn't even wince. She didn't want to give him any indication that he had hurt her in any way after what had just transpired with the rocking chair.

"Hurry up," he commanded her to finish her food.

"I don't know if I can finish the food because of this," she said quietly.

"I said that you will finish your food. You don't have a choice," he barked.

Without looking up, Lareina rapidly shoveled the last bits of food down. The quicker she could get Tony out of the cabin, the sooner she could get working on her project.

Tony grabbed the plate and fork from her tiny hands. He threw them in to an old sink that clearly had not been used in decades.

"Just for all this, you will scrub all the floors, clean all the dishes, and wash all of our clothes when I return. Is that clear?"

"Yes, sir." Lareina replied, her head hanging low.

Tony quickly got up, grabbed his coat and hurriedly left the cabin.

After Lareina heard the car start and drive way she whispered, "oh thank God!"

She slowly pulled her beaten and bruised body up and shuffled back into the main room of the cabin. Painfully, she reached down into her pocket and picked out the material with her swollen hands. "What can I do with you?" She asked the fabric, as if it would speak to her. She looked around for inspiration. Looking at the floor, she found a large nail that was coming up out of the floor. "Perfect!" She exclaimed, not even realizing the volume from her excitement.

Lareina placed the material down on the floor and began to pull up the nail. Her small swollen hands slipped on the cold, hard, ancient nail. This would not be an easy undertaking, especially with her hands and ankles still bound. Lareina considered cutting the tape with the nail head, but she feared that her attempt to rebind her hands later would be too obvious to Tony. As much as she hated struggling like this, she knew she couldn't have him suspect anything.

Determined, Lareina grabbed the nail again and pulled upwards with all of her might. She was able to get it up and out of the floor further but she fell backwards from pulling with such force. With a deep breath, Lareina slowly rolled herself back onto her knees and grasped the nail again. Once more she pulled with what little strength she had. The nail was becoming looser, but she still had more work to do.

Lareina did not know how long it took her to finally extract the nail from the floor, but eventually she held it in her hands. She quickly but painfully picked up the material as well and scuffled back into the kitchen as quickly as she could. She knew that Tony had a hammer somewhere: she remembered seeing it on more than one occasion. She quickly went through all the drawers. After quickly scanning several drawers, she found the hammer.

With the three tools carefully balanced in her small, swollen, bound hands, Lareina scurried out of the cabin and back to her tree.

She looked at her carving work. She was still very proud of how well she had done with that. Now, she needed to add to her handy work. This project, however, would be far more difficult than carving into the tree.

She rose to her tip toes. Instantly, she already felt weak and light headed. She knew there was no way she could expend more energy in her weak state. Slowly and carefully she brought herself back down and she placed the hammer, nail and fabric on the ground. She quickly shuffled to the river and gulped as much water as she could. With her hands bound and swollen, it was difficult to get a decent amount of water in her hands. She took in as many small gulps as she could. Lareina knew that the starvation and dehydration she had been enduring for all of these days was finally catching up to her. This endeavor could very well possibly be her last attempt to save herself, but she had to try. She'd rather die trying than to give in to a monster like Tony.

After taking in as much water as possible, Lareina stood back up and trekked back up to her tree.

Weakly, she grabbed her materials. She held the fabric and placed it into her "x" shaped carving. She took the nail and held it as close to the top of the fabric as her short arms would reach. Lareina took her first swing with the hammer. It was too much for her painful, swollen hands. Everything came crashing down on her.

Weak and exhausted, Lareina began to cry. This was so difficult. It was so discouraging and such an atrocious situation for her to be in. She hated this cabin and these woods. She so desperately wanted to go home. Why hadn't anyone found her yet? She had sent them such great information already, and yet here she was struggling to give them another clue because they still hadn't found her! Lareina simply could not understand why she had not yet been rescued. Was it possible that she had been forgotten or even presumed her dead? Would her family and friends give up on her that quickly and easily? She hoped not, but she knew that it was a possibility. She could not fight back the tears of fear and frustration any longer. She sat on the ground and cried for several minutes.

"No," she sniffled to herself. "I can't give up now. I have to do this." Picking herself up and gingerly handling the tools she placed the material into her carving; the nail fairly close to the top of the fabric, and she took a small swing. With her arm movements so limited she would have to make small, but strong swings in order to get the nail to stay into the thick, deep bark of the tree.

Swing after tiny swing, Lareina finally began to notice progress. She had been hammering for nearly an eternity when the nail and material finally sat well in the tree. For precautionary reasons she swung the hammer a few more times, just to ensure that her "flag" would not be lost.

With sweat pouring down her face, she marveled at her own ingenuity. She was far more resourceful than even she ever imagined. She was quite proud of her "x" and of her little "flag."

A significant amount of time had passed. The day had slipped away while Lareina hammered in her flag. Her body felt weak and depleted after that expulsion of energy. In order to help her body Lareina slowly shuffled back down to the river again, and drank some more water out of her sore and swollen hands.

After several small drinks, she hesitantly made her way back into the cabin so that Tony wouldn't notice anything unusual. She wasn't sure how long this project had taken her, and she couldn't be sure how much more sweet solitude she could enjoy before he finally returned.

Marc stared intensely at the two notes from Lareina. "X marks the spot. Large tree; walking path. Merced River, north of Ele-." The Merced River was where Marc and the other officers had been searching. No one had found an "x." Was this a new sign she had put up since they had ventured up that way? Had they missed a clear marking to her location? And what was Ele? E – l – e. What on Earth could that stand for?

Marc decided to call the Oliveiras, Lareina's parents.

"¿Hola?"

"Mrs. Oliveira?"

"Yes?"

"My name is Detective Raymer, I am with the LAPD. I'm working on your daughter's kidnapping."

The woman on the other end of the phone began hysterically crying. "She's dead, isn't she?"

"No ma'am. At least, not that we know of.

"We actually got another text message from her."

Mrs. Oliveira was clearly trying to control her overwhelming emotions. "Oh thank God! She is such a smart and resourceful girl."

"Yes, that much I do know. But there are a few things I don't know. I have a few questions for you if you don't mind."

"No, not at all. That is fine, Detective."

"Mrs. Oliveira, does 'E – l - e' mean anything in Spanish?"

"No Detective."

"Was it a pet name for her? Something special to her or the family? Possibly even a nickname for Sandy or someone else close to her?"

"Ummm...no. Not that I know of."

"Hmmmm...ok.

"Does your family have any property or any special places up along the Merced River?"

"No, not at all. But we - her father, brother and I – we do live up near there. We live in Redwood City."

"You do?"

"Yes we do, Detective. When my husband retired he decided he wanted to leave Los Angeles, so we all moved up here except for Lareina."

"Oh, ok. That's good to know. Thank you for telling me that, it may be helpful to us in the case.

"And now you're sure there's nothing in or near the Yosemite area that would mean anything to her or the family?"

"No. There's nothing that I can imagine, sir. Not at all. I'm so sorry."

"No, don't apologize Mrs. Oliveira. You have been more than helpful. I want you to know we are working on this case night and day. I will not rest until we bring your daughter home."

"Thank you so much, Detective. I appreciate it."

"You're welcome, Mrs. Oliveira. Please do not hesitate to call me at any time day or night, if you think of anything."

"I won't. Many thanks."

"You're welcome. Take care. We'll be in touch soon."

Marc hung up, still confused. As endless thoughts swirled around his mind, he realized Oswald had never called him back yesterday about the coordinates from the cryptic message. He decided to call back up to him to see what he could learn.

"Hello?" It sounded like Brian's voice this time.

"Brian?"

"Yes?"

"Brian, it's Marcus."

"Oh heya, Marc. What's up?"

"Brian, can you please review those coordinates with me in the Oliveira case?"

"Yeah, hang on." Brian put the phone down while he picked up the case file. "Ok, what do you want to know?"

"Brian, what are the coordinates you have written down? The ones we were sent out to?"

"Well, let me look here. I have coordinates of north thirty seven degrees and forty five minutes, and west one hundred nineteen degrees and fifteen minutes."

"But Brian, it was north thirty seven degrees forty four minutes and west one hundred nineteen degrees and approximately forty minutes."

"Wait, what?"

"Yes! I'm not kidding, Brian. North thirty seven degrees forty four minutes and west one hundred nineteen degrees and approximately forty minutes."

"Oh shit! Marc, I'm sorry. I seriously screwed that one up."

"Brian, are you fucking kidding me?!"

"No Marc. I'm not. I must have copied the numbers down wrong. I'm sorry. I am truly sorry."

"Damn it," Marc paused for a moment, and took a deep breath. "Regardless, do you have any idea what 'E – l - e' could be in relation to all this?"

"Well, you guys were searching just below Elephant Rock, right? Maybe it's supposed to be that. E – l - e would seem like a logical start to the word elephant."

"True enough. Elephant Rock. Ok. And you said we were South of that?"

"Yeah, based on my screw up."

"Shit. She just sent us a text message saying that she was north of Elephant Rock or whatever that is."

"Maybe her battery was dying or the guy found her or something and that was all she could enter, Marc.

"It sounds like you guys were close, but probably just on the wrong side of the river."

"Damn it," Marc whispered.

"Marcus, I am so sorry."

"It's ok, Brian. Shit happens. I just have to call Karl now and see if he'd be willing to dispatch another search party.

"First and foremost, I will need an exact map of the correct coordinates, ok? We need to know exactly where she is. Karl won't give me anything until I have it pinpointed exactly."

"Yeah, no problem. I'll search it on the computer and print you out an exact map. I'll get that to you as soon as I can. It's my top priority now, Marc.

"As for Karl – shit. I am sorry, man. Look, if he gives you any problems have him call me. I fucked this one up, and I won't let this girl die on account of my mistake."

"Thanks, Brian. Much appreciated."

Marc hung up and buried his face in his hands. How could all this be happening? He had been right all along. They had been close to her, but they narrowly missed the target. Marc could not believe they had been so close and yet so far from saving Lareina. So much time had been lost! They needed to get back up there and search for her immediately. Marc was frustrated, excited and confused all at once.

He couldn't let his emotions get the best of him. Not now. Now they were truly close to saving her. Marc sat up, gathered his thoughts and continued on his quest to save Lareina.

Tony finally arrived back at the cabin. Lareina looked up from the floor. She had fallen asleep due to her exhaustion.

Tony threw the bag of sanitary napkins and tampons at her. "Go fix yourself."

"Yes," she quietly responded. Slowly, she rose and took the bag and scuffled out to the woods. While behind a tree, she stuck a sanitary pad and a wrapper on the tree. She opened the box of tampons next. She took one out of the box and threw it as far into the woods as she could. She did so just to appease Tony and make him believe her farce.

With all the courage she could muster, Lareina slowly walked back to the cabin. She was greeted by Tony with a handful of plates and his clothing.

"I did my part, now it's your time to hold up your end of the bargain. Scrub all of these – well. The bleach and scrub brush will be waiting for you when you come back inside."

"Yes Tony," she mumbled.

Tony pulled out his knife and cut the tape frighteningly close to Lareina's wrist. He then handed her the pile.

With her head down, Lareina walked down to the river to begin washing everything as best she could. She didn't have much time. The sun was beginning to set over the horizon of the river. It took every ounce of strength, but she scrubbed diligently. The plates looked clean: Lareina could not find one speck of food on them, so she figured they should be satisfactory to Tony. The clothes were as clean as they were ever going to be.

Lareina made her way back to the cabin and laid out the clothes on the porch railing. She brought the plates back to Tony inside. She immediately sat down and began scrubbing the floor with the bleach and brush. She scrubbed as hard as she could until she nearly fell over from exhaustion.

She knew it was going to be another long, torturous night with Tony in the cabin as he came back in to examine her cleaning work.

Chapter 14

Lareina could not sleep. Though her body was weak and exhausted, sleep eluded her. For hours on end she lay on the blanket squeezing her eyes shut, hoping that she would just slip away into dream land and forget this horrid reality. It didn't work. Just before dawn she got up, brought the clothes in and folded them so Tony would be pleased.

After folding the clothes for him, she lay back down hoping to get at least a few hours of rest. Soon after she lay down, sleep finally came.

Lareina and Tony were jolted awake by a sudden loud mass of noise. Cars could be heard pulling up all around the cabin, as could police sirens. Was it possible that Lareina would finally be rescued today? Her heart leaped at the thought.

Tony jumped up and looked out the window. There were several patrol and unmarked police cars surrounding the tiny cabin. "Shit!" He exclaimed.

He grabbed the blankets and clothes, and threw them into the kitchen, hoping that no one would snoop around.

He then dragged Lareina into a tiny closet she hadn't even noticed before. He held her in the dark closet with his fat hand over her mouth. With his other hand, he pulled out his knife and held it against her neck. He held it tightly with the razor sharp edge digging into her skin. "If you so much as sneeze, I will kill you!" His hot breath whispered in her ear.

With her pulse racing Lareina did her best so as to not move, to not even breathe too hard. Her life was truly on the line, and she refused to die now when she was so close to salvation.

The cabin door creaked open. Several pairs of foot steps could be heard entering the tiny abode. The floor squeaked all around them. Lareina fought to steady her breathing.

After what felt to be an infinite amount of time, someone finally spoke.

"So this is the place, huh?" It was a man's voice. Not one that Lareina recognized.

"Ashley, sweetheart, is this where the bad man took you?" It was a woman's voice. The tone in her voice indicated a motherly, nurturing personality. She sounded like she might have been the mother or some other close relative to this Ashley girl.

Lareina was confused. Who else would have known about this cabin? How or why would anyone else have ever come here? Who was this Ashley person? Why were all these police here, but not for her?

Lareina's heart sank when she finally realized that yet another day would pass without rescue.

They could hear a little girl moan, and the floor then screeched. Lareina imagined some poor young little girl burying herself into her mommy's leg after returning to such a bad place.

The little girl began crying and whimpering.

Without even thinking Lareina reached out, as if to go help the poor child. As she did so she could feel Tony press the knife harder against her neck. He actually pierced her skin. Lareina could feel one little drop of blood trickle down her neck. She slowly pulled back, and then stood motionlessly.

"It's ok, sweetheart. The bad man isn't here. You're safe with Mommy," the woman's voice tenderly reassured the child.

"I take all this to mean yes," the man said.

"Yes, Sergeant. It has to.

"This is exactly how she described the place to me. Different places don't normally bother her like this. I'm sure this is it."

"Ashley," the man's voice was soft and caring. "Is this where the bad man took you and did all those bad things?"

"Mmmm hmmm," the little voice groaned.

"Was this the only room in the cabin he took you?" The Sergeant was very kind, caring and patient with his tiny victim.

"Yeah," Ashley's little voice said weakly.

"Ok," he said. "Thank you."

"Sergeant, may I take her outside? Just to give her some kind of reprieve? Please?"

"Oh, absolutely, Mrs. Robinson."

The steps of both the mother and child could be heard leaving the cabin followed by the door creaking shut.

"This place is pretty far hidden. This guy went out of his way to do this," a new man spoke.

"No shit, Smith," the first man's voice replied. "But Dominick Covelli has always been smart. He knows how to hide his shit.

"The one thing I don't get is why he brought every one of the girls here."

"This place has to hold some kind of meaning to him."

"Well obviously, Smith! He just makes it easier for us every time. Now we know where to look. They say criminals aren't smart, and he's the epitome of that!

"Ya know Smith, after this one he's gonna be locked up for life. With a record like his, he's fucked."

"Who cares?! He's a damn child molester, Serge."

"A child molester with an obvious pattern.

"I just wonder how many more are out there that aren't speaking up – ya know the ones we don't know about."

"I know it. But at least with this one, he can't hurt any more kids."

"No shit!

"Hey Smith, did you see that car parked a ways back out there?"

"The 'Stang? Yeah. Why?"

"Remember that Detective coming up from L. A. looking for an old Mustang just like that one?"

"Oh yeah! Shit, I forgot about him."

"We can't forget about him or that case. We need to check that out before we go, too. Make sure you write down the plate number. It supposedly belongs to Covelli's brother."

"No shit, Serge!"

"Yeah, Smith. This is serious. If it is his, then we really have to look into this. Their entire family could have some weird tie to this place."

"Ok, Serge. Will do.

"Do we need to look around here for anything before I go get that plate number?"

"No, Smith. Just get the CSI team in here to take pictures of the Cabin: inside and out."

"Ok, boss."

Smith walked out of the cabin and within moments, several new pairs of foot steps could be heard entering and walking around.

Suddenly, flashes of light from a camera flash were oozing into the closet from the floor. Various voices were heard speaking softly while the CSI team took their pictures and collected any other possible evidence.

Lareina had never held her breath for so long while she and Tony waited for the CSI team and the Sergeant to finally leave the building. It felt like an eternity, but after a while the CSI team began to finally leave the cabin.

Tony still held her in the closet. Neither of them moved. They each fought to control their breathing, and sweat poured from Tony's forehead. The cars had yet to start up though, and Tony refused to move until he knew the cops were long gone.

What Tony didn't understand was why it would take the police so long to copy down his plate number. Unbeknownst to Tony, Smith had found the sanitary napkin and wrapper stuck to a tree. As he and the Sergeant examined that, another officer called out saying that he had found an unused tampon amongst the leaves. The Sergeant ordered the CSI team to collect the napkin, wrapper and tampon as evidence and to test them for any epithelial cells or DNA.

After over an hour or two of excruciating anxiety, cars finally began starting up and pulling away. Several minutes of nothingness had passed and Tony figured it was safe to exit the tiny, pitch black closet.

He opened the closet door and pushed Lareina forward. She fell onto her hands and knees.

"You little fucking bitch! You called them! You led them here!"

Lareina looked up at Tony. "No, Tony! I didn't. Come on, you heard them: they were here because of that little girl."

"Fucking Dominick," Tony said walking away.

"Dominick?"

"Yeah."

"Who is that?"

"That's my brother."

"Your brother? But that was a little child!"

"Yeah, I know. The fucker can't keep his hands off little girls.

"That jackass just made parole, and now he's about to be locked up for life because of this one. What a fucking dumbass!"

"So, all of that was true?"

"Yeah, unfortunately. Goddamn idiot can't keep it in his pants when it comes to pre-pubescent girls."

Lareina didn't move from her position on the floor, for fear it might startle or anger Tony more. He was clearly at a level of high stress and anxiety; Lareina could only imagine what her sudden movements might cause him to do. She dared not say or do anything that would set him off.

"We have to do something. We're not safe here any more. We have to get out of here," Tony said with a tone or urgency in his voice.

"Where would we go, Tony?"

"What difference does it make to you, bitch?"

Tony pulled Lareina up by her hair and threw her backwards. She fell on her back. He walked up to her. He could see the fear in her gorgeous hazel eyes. He kicked her in the ribs. Lareina rolled over into a fetal position from the pain.

"Get up!" He ordered her.

Writhing in such excruciating pain Lareina moved very slowly.

"I said, get up!" Tony again pulled Lareina up by her thick black locks. She wobbled as he tried to steady her on her feet. Seeing her physically weakened, he slapped her. Blood began to drip from her mouth. Not wanting another endless floor scrubbing session, Lareina quickly used her sleeve to dab the blood. Slowly she turned and looked at Tony.

Without even batting an eye, Tony punched Lareina and she went flying backwards. Lareina fell into a wall and then slid down to the floor.

Tony began walking towards her. Lareina had little energy to fight, but she also feared this was the beginning of the end of her life.

As Tony approached, Lareina stood up. She charged at him. With all her might, she punched him in the stomach. She didn't feel strong, but Lareina was mightier than she realized. Tony curled down into a ball from the pain.

Lareina ran out of the cabin as quickly as she could. She frantically looked for tire marks from the police cars. She found a weak set, and began to follow them away from the cabin as best she could. She prayed that the uneven terrain would slow the cars down enough that she could catch up to them.

Lareina ran with what little strength and energy she had. Her body was incredibly weak. She hardly any strength left, but she knew she needed to survive. With endless pain from all of the bruises, wounds, and cuts that covered her body, she continued to run in the car tracks as quickly as possible. She had no idea if Tony had even followed her. Lareina dared not look back, for fear she might fall down and lose precious time, or worse: get recaptured.

The ground was wet and uneven underneath Lareina's small, weak feet. Her gate was unsteady because of the terrain but Lareina pushed herself forward, in the hopes of being saved. Step by step her pace slowed, but she still ran with as much strength as she could muster as she followed the tracks left by the police vehicles.

Suddenly, she was lifted up of the ground from behind. Tony had caught up to her and grabbed her by the back of her shirt. Lareina moved, kicked and tried to wiggle her way out of his grasp on her.

As quickly as he picked her up, Tony unexpectedly dropped her face first into the dirt.

Lareina quickly rolled over and watched as Tony loomed over her. She scrambled to move backwards. Her hands and feet slipped, she hardly moved at all.

Lareina tried to kick Tony in the crotch, but as she brought her leg up, her body fell back onto the dirt, rocks and leaves.

He grabbed her by the arm and pulled her up ruthlessly.

Lareina could no longer fight back the tears. For the first time, she allowed Tony to see her emotions get the best of her.

"Oh, you're just scared," Tony's demeanor changed completely in a second. "Don't cry, honey," he whispered as he wiped away a tear. "It's going to be ok. We'll be safe, I promise. I won't let them hurt us."

Lareina could not understand this man at all. First, he nearly tries to kill her, now he was promising to protect her. His lack of predictability only added to her fears.

Tony put his arm around Lareina's shoulder, and slowly the two walked back to the cabin.

As they re-entered the confining cabin, Tony said, "We're going to have to get rid of the car. And we definitely have to get the hell out of here. Otherwise, they'll find us and keep us apart."

Tony took his car keys and began to walk back out to the Mustang.

"Wait!" Lareina cried out.

"What?" Tony turned around, surprised at Lareina's call out to him. He looked at her with a perplexed expression.

"All of my belongings are in the car, Tony."

"So?"

"So, if you let me take them out, we can carry as much food as we can pack into my purse."

Tony was astonished and impressed by Lareina's thinking. "That's not a bad idea," he said. He tightly gripped Lareina's arm and dragged her out to the car.

Tony had purposefully parked the Mustang a significant distance away from the cabin in the hopes that no one would find it or make the connection to the cabin. It was too late for that now, though. He couldn't let them find it again.

Lareina fought to keep up with Tony's uninjured and rapid walking pace. They marched over the uneven terrain of the forest towards the now infamous Mustang. Tony had a good lead over Lareina's debilitated pace, but she followed him without muttering any complaints.

They reached the old car at last.

Tony lifted open the hatch back and Lareina grabbed her bag.

No sooner had Lareina taken her belongings that Tony hopped into the car and put it into neutral.

"You steer," he barked at her.

"Why don't we just drive it down to the river, Tony?"

"I don't want to risk anyone hearing it, in case the cops are still around or something."

Hesitantly, Lareina sighed and got into the car. She tried to steer as Tony pushed the car through the muck and mire of the forest heading down towards the river.

Since the car was so far from the river, both Tony and Lareina battled to keep the car moving towards the river. Tony pushed as hard as he could. He used his fat weight to keep the car moving forward. Lareina struggled to keep the car headed in the right direction. She grasped the steering wheel as tightly as she could but her damaged hands fought to maintain control over it. It was strenuous for both of them as they inched the car step by step to the river. Both Tony and Lareina used every ounce of strength they had. It didn't take long for each of them to be sweating profusely. This was an excruciating undertaking.

An indefinite amount of time had passed by the time they reached the river bank. Tony stopped pushing, and Lareina got out of the car.

"I hate to do this. I've had this car for years - it's all I have," Tony said out of breath. "But I have to, in order to save us."

Lareina remained silent.

Tony wiped the sweat from his brow. He stared at his beloved old car. He was still out of breath, and the thought of drowning his car caused him to struggle for air even more so.

Tony knew he couldn't be emotional right now; he had to focus on survival. He gathered himself back together. Reluctantly, he got behind the car again and pushed it into the cold river. The two watched silently as the car slowly sank into its watery grave.

Tony sighed. "Well, that's one less thing to worry about. At least now they can't track the car."

The sun had nearly completely set on the river's horizon. Yet another day was gone.

In utter silence, Tony and Lareina walked back to the cabin.

Chapter 15

Unable to sleep, the Oliveiras decided to drive to find any sign of their daughter. Their lack of any direct communication with her, and the fact that they had not spoken with Detective Raymer in a few days were eating them alive. They knew the police were working hard, but they wanted more. They felt so helpless and isolated during this entire process, it only seemed right that they also searched for their beloved child.

For hours, they drove around in the dark around the city of Fresno, and then finally they headed east. They were soon lost in a sea of trees and nothingness. There were no landmarks, nor any signs of civilization or life. They drove endlessly, in the hopes that they might catch a glimpse of their daughter.

As they drove around and strained to see in the opaque night sky, Jose Oliveira thought he saw something. "Stop!" He shouted.

Consuelo slammed on the brakes. They were both jolted by the abrupt stop. "What is it, Jose?"

"Look," he said, pointing out his window. There before them stood an ominous tree, with a large "x" carved into it. A piece of fabric dangled from within the "x." It was an unusual and frightening display. Both Jose and Consuelo shivered from the sight.

"What do you think that is, Jose? Do you think that could be from Lareina?" Consuelo asked her husband.

"Yes I do, Consuelo. Think about it. X is her letter. It's all that algebra stuff.

"I'd bet you anything that this is a sign that she was here."

"Well if you think so, then take a picture with your phone!" Consuelo demanded of her husband.

"You do it. You know I don't know how to operate this stupid thing," Jose responded handing the phone over to Consuelo.

Consuelo got out of the car with Jose's phone in hand. She walked up to the tree, and angled her head upwards. She could nearly break her neck looking up at such a tall tree. She wondered how on Earth her daughter could have created such a sizable and significantly deep mark in a tree of this size.

She aimed the phone camera up towards the "x" and the fabric. Unsure how good of a picture she'd get, Consuelo took multiple pictures of the sight before her, hoping that it would help the police to locate Lareina.

Consuelo ran back into the car and immediately called Detective Raymer.

"Hello?" His voice was groggy and scratchy. It was only then that Consuelo realized it was after two in the morning.

"Detective Raymer?"

"Yes?"

"Sir, it's Consuelo Oliveira, Lareina's mother."

"Oh, hello Mrs. Oliveira," Marc said as he clearly stretched. "What can I do for you at this hour of the night?"

"Detective, I think my husband and I have some information about our daughter's whereabouts."

"What?! Really?! Please, do tell me."

"We could not sleep, Detective. This is just tearing us up so much. We decided we needed to see what we could do.

"So, we've been driving for hours and hours now. We're somewhere in a forest, and we found a tree with an 'x' carved into it, and there is also a piece of fabric hanging from the 'x.' We're not sure, but we think it's a sign Lareina was there.

"I took some pictures with my husband's phone."

140

"Very good!" Marc said with great enthusiasm. "Can you come into the office at 9:00 am sharp tomorrow, so you can show me those pictures? We need to see exactly what it looks like.

"This very well could easily help us to find her, Mrs. Oliveira."

"Yes, of course we'll be there! Oh, I hope you're right Detective! That is such wonderful news!"

"Indeed it is. Thank you so much for doing this."

"Sir, this is my daughter. I'd do anything for her."

"I know you would.

"Try to get some sleep, and I'll see you at nine."

"Sounds wonderful, Detective. Thank you."

"Thank you, Mrs. Oliveira."

Marc hung up. He lay in bed, unable to go back to sleep. Images of what the Oliveiras might have seen raced through his mind. An "x" carved into a tree with some fabric attached to it. The idea of a real sign from Lareina being seen was phenomenal to Marc. The thought that he could be so close in finding Lareina excited him far too much for him to sleep. Instead, he continually imagined her rescue for the rest of the night.

The pictures were dark and showed little. Marc strained to see the tree on the phone's tiny screen.

"I know these aren't great, Detective, but it's all we have," Consuelo said, fighting back her tears.

"I understand, Mrs. Oliveira. You did an excellent job. No need to worry.

"In fact, I'm going to hook up the cable, download the pictures and print them out. They could be very useful to us, Mrs. Oliveira.

"I am in awe. Thank you so much for finding this."

"I'm happy to help," she said while tears streamed down her refined but worn face. Lareina had clearly acquired her beauty from her mother, but the strain of this situation was taking an obvious toll on Consuelo.

"Now," Marc said. "Lareina had sent us a message that said, 'X Marcs the spot. Large tree; walking path. Merced River, north of Ele -.' Do you have any inkling as to what that might mean in relation to this tree you found last night?"

"Well, let's see. We were over by the Merced River. We could have been on a walking path – we drove anywhere and everywhere we could. So, we're not sure exactly where we were," Consuelo replied.

"Were you north of Elephant Rock?"

"We're just not sure, Detective." Jose answered.

"Ok, that's fine.

"Please excuse me for just one moment," Detective Raymer said as he rose to get the phone adapter.

A few minutes later, Marc returned with the phone cable in hand. He plugged it in to his computer and to Mr. Oliveira's phone.

The pictures quickly loaded up, and then Marc's printer went to work printing out larger versions of the dim images.

While the Oliveiras and Marc waited for all of the pictures to print, Marc's phone rang.

"Detective Raymer."

"Detective, my name is Joanna Palmer. I am a CSI investigator in Fresno."

"Ok. What can I do for you, Miss Palmer?"

"Detective, some of the local officers here were working on another case, and they found an unused tampon scattered in the woods on the North side of the Merced River."

"Ok? And what exactly what does that have to do with me, Miss Palmer?"

"Detective Raymer, we found epithelial cells with DNA that matches the DNA of your missing person, Lareina Oliveira."

"Really?! Please, tell me more."

"There's not much to tell.

"All I can say is that the cells are a match. The tampon was found randomly in the woods, we don't know how long it was out there, although the condition seemed fairly good – almost new."

"Ok, so it probably wasn't out there too long."

"It would seem so, Detective Raymer. My guess is that it probably wasn't out there too long. Less than a week, I'm sure."

"And what was the case you were working on, Miss Palmer?"

"I'm sorry, Detective. I am not at liberty to say.

"Our Chief of police is more than willing to meet and speak with you, though, Detective."

"Ok. Let him know I'll be leaving Los Angeles as quickly as I can. Hopefully, I'll arrive there in about five hours or so."

"Ok, sir. I will tell him."

"Wonderful. Thank you, Ms. Palmer."

Marc hung up.

"What was that about, Detective?" The normally quiet Jose Oliveira asked with excitement and nervousness in his voice.

"An item of evidence with Lareina's DNA was found on the North side of the Merced River."

Consuelo began to cry.

"Don't cry, Mrs. Oliveira. This is actually good. Really good.

"More than likely, she is still alive, and is trying to send us a sign."

Mrs. Oliveira looked up at Marc through her tears. "Do you truly think so?"

"Yes, ma'am, I do.

"Look, I need to head up to Fresno for this. Do you both need a ride back home?"

"No, we took our car," Jose answered.

"Ok, just follow me up, and I'll have a police escort take you all the way home to Redwood City."

"Ok, Detective. Thank you," Jose said.

Within only a few minutes, Marc and the Oliveiras were headed back up north, towards Fresno.

Lareina pushed the food around on her paper plate. She was overwhelmed with depression and fatigue. She had so greatly hoped for salvation yesterday, but yet she remained Tony's prisoner. Her heart literally felt like it had sunk within her body. Negative thoughts and feelings swirled around in her mind like a tornado. She found it was impossible for her muster up the ability to eat when she was so engulfed by sorrow.

"You have to eat, honey," Tony said gently, breaking the silence of the morning. "You'll need all the strength and energy possible. We have to find a new place to live today."

Lareina was greatly sickened by Tony's presence. She hated him with every inch of her being. She fully despised this situation. Instead of focusing on saving herself, all she could feel was self-pity and a deep loathing for Tony. She so desperately wanted to get away from him, and from this horrendous place. She longed to be home with her friends and family. She wanted her normal life back, and she greatly wished Tony was dead.

He began to massage her shoulders. She turned away from him. She could feel his filth sneaking its way into her body. It felt as though it was being absorbed by her pores, and covering her like a slimy blanket. Lareina thought about how she could bathe and scrub endlessly and she still would not be able to wash Tony's foulness off of herself.

Lareina turned back to her food, hoping that if she did Tony would take his dirty hands off of her. She slowly nibbled at the tiny pieces of nondescript food bits.

"That's a good girl," Tony said as he continued to touch her.

"So, tell me about your case, Chief," Marc said to Chief Wilmont, the Fresno Chief of police.

"Well, as you may remember, I told you there's a registered sex offender here in town named Dominick Covelli."

"Yes, I do remember you mentioning that the last time we met."

"Well Detective Raymer, we had another young girl come forward and she led us to a cabin on the North side of the river.

"While we were searching the area, we found a car similar to the one that you had that APB on. And we also found an unused tampon in the woods with Lareina's DNA on it."

"Was there any blood on the Tampon? Any other signs from her? Any indications of a struggle?"

"And as far as the car goes, what can you tell me?"

"Here's what we've got Detective: no blood on the tampon or anywhere else that we could see. There were no signs of a struggle. No signs of life, either. No foot prints, no nothing.

"It just happened to be a bizarre coincidence that we found the car and the tampon.

"Now as far as the car goes, I asked one of my officers to run the plate number but I haven't heard anything back."

"Call him."

"I will, Detective Raymer."

"No, I mean call him now. We have to know if that's the car. And if it is, I want to get there as quickly as possible."

"Ok, Detective. Hold on for just one minute here."

Chief Wilmont picked up his phone desk and dialed a number.

"Smith?"

"Yes, Chief?"

"What do you have on the license plates from that Mustang near the Covelli cabin?"

"Oh...ummm....hang on, Chief."

Smith put the phone down and could be heard searching his desk frantically.

"Uhhh...Chief, can I call you back on that one?"

"Why? What's wrong, Smith?"

"I...uhhh...I can't find the plate number. I know I wrote it down. It's got to be here somewhere."

"You can't find the plate number?!"

"It's here; I know it is, Chief. My desk is just really cluttered or I'm looking in the wrong place. I do have it, I promise. I just need to find it and..."

"Smith, are you telling me that you haven't even called that one in yet?"

"Uhhh...no, Chief. I have not."

"And why the hell not?!"

"Well...uhhh...Chief, it's just that I've been really swamped."

"God damn it, Smith! That's no excuse! You know how important both of these Covelli cases are!"

"I know. I'm sorry, Chief. I really am! I'll get right on it. As soon as I can find the plate number, I assure you!"

"God damn it, Smith!"

Chief Wilmont slammed down the phone.

"I'm sorry, Detective Raymer. I don't have any more information for you. My officer really dropped the ball on this one. I'm sorry."

"Chief, I don't have time for this bullshit. Take me to where you found that car – now!"

Lareina was in the kitchen, she packed as much of the food as she could in her little purse. As she shoved crackers and other small foods into her bag, she watched out of the corner of her eye that Tony had rolled up one of the blankets. He also carried the roll of electrical tape on his arm. It was an ominous reminder to Lareina.

They both looked around the cabin one last time before they left. It was quiet, it was sinister. Lareina felt a pang of sadness. She feared that since they'd now be mobile she had absolutely no hope of being rescued. This quiet moment brought her great anxiety and grief.

"I hate to leave our home honey, but it's what we have to do," Tony muttered.

They put their shoes on and left the cabin. Tony tightly held Lareina's painful little hand as he began walking east, deeper into the woods.

Lareina tripped frequently and slowly trudged behind Tony as they wandered through the forest. She felt hopeless. She knew that her chances of being found were diminishing by the second. Yet, she had to follow Tony or else he might truly kill her. She could not imagine a worse predicament.

They wandered with no particular destination or direction. The trees all looked the same to Lareina. How would she ever be found? There were no landmarks or signs that the police could use to find her now. Lareina's fears increased as the sun sank lower and lower in the sky.

Tonight, she'd be sleeping out in the woods – if she was lucky. They walked all day and Tony wasn't showing any signs of slowing down. Lareina knew that there was a strong possibility that they may not sleep at all tonight. She still fought to catch up to Tony. There were times during their excursion where her short arm was stretched to its limit as he insisted on holding on to her, and she was unable to keep up with his pace.

Realizing her greatest fears and that a short distance had started to come between them while her arm was stretched further and further, Lareina forced herself to catch up to Tony. They continued to walk through the dark forest in an eerie silence.

Chapter 16

Although the night sky had fallen like a thick, black velvet curtain, the area was bright with flood lights and the flashing blue and red lights from all the police vehicles.

There was nothing to be seen but trees, trees, and more trees.

"Are you sure that this is the location where you found the car?" Marc impatiently asked Chief Wilmont.

"Yes Detective Raymer. This was definitely the spot. I'm sorry. I swear to you, it was here.

"Somehow, he must have found out that we spotted it and either took it or dumped it somewhere."

"Where the hell would he go, Chief Wilmont? There's an APB on that damn car! He has to know he couldn't drive it anywhere!

"And where would he dump it? There's nothing around here. There's no place to dump a car and not have it be seen!" Marc's stress and frustration had gotten the better of him. Lareina had been missing for so many days. There was no reason why she should not have been found by now. Marc began to pace.

"Detective Raymer, you are asking questions I can't answer. God only knows.

"You and I both see there's nothing here. They could be anywhere."

"Look Chief, I want a crew out here to start searching for any tire tracks, foot prints or otherwise. And I want them out here now, do you understand?" Marc was firm in his demands.

"Detective, there's no way I can dispatch a team out here at this hour. We don't even know where we are."

"I don't care! I don't want any excuses! A young woman has been missing for far too long, Chief Wilmont. We need to bring her home, if she's still alive. And if not, we need to get her a proper burial.

"Time is not on our side. Now get me CSI, some canine units and patrol officers out here immediately. I refuse to let Lareina Oliveira stay missing any longer."

Lareina and Tony continued to walk through the forest without any direction throughout the night. The forest was incredibly dark: it was a wonder they weren't walking in circles with such limited visibility.

Their trek was exhausting. They had taken only a few breaks, and Lareina was starting to feel as though her body did not have the stamina to keep up with Tony's swift pace.

Unaware of Lareina's exhaustion, Tony maintained a brisk walk as they marched deeper and deeper into the woods. He refused to allow the police to find them. He was so determined that he would not rest until he felt they were safe and secluded.

As their hike went on, whenever possible, Lareina would secretly take a small item like a pen, a piece of paper, or anything other than their food from her bag and drop it onto the ground. She hoped that despite the strong and bitingly cold winds and woodland life, that she was leaving a trail for someone to somehow come and rescue her. She felt as if it was a parallel to the story of Hansel and Gretel, but it was the only hope she currently had to that could help lead people to her.

In silence, the pair sustained their trek through the dark, shadowy woods; hearing only the sounds of their own footsteps and that of the near by wildlife. Lareina knew there would be no rest tonight as she passed by domineering tree after dark, domineering tree. Gathering up all the strength she could, she slowly walked behind Tony into the darkness.

Marc looked all around for tire tracks. The dirt looked as if there had been some kind of movement, but he could not confirm any tread marks.

The sun was finally starting to come up. As Marc watched the sunrise, he noticed the amazing reflection in the river. It was a striking sight. The river twinkled and glittered with sunlight. Suddenly, an idea came to him.

Marc turned to the Fresno Chief, who was clearly exhausted from the chaos and seemingly endless work from the night. "How quickly can you get an underwater team here?"

Wearily, Chief Wilmont looked up at Marc. "What?! Are you fucking kidding me, Raymer?"

"No Chief. I want this river searched thoroughly. I don't want to miss anything.

"You said yourself last night that Tony might have dumped the car. What if he dumped it in the river? It could be right in front of us and we don't even know it! We have to look for it in there. You and I both know this is a damn good possibility."

"Damn it, Raymer. Do you have any idea what you're asking for here?"

"Chief Wilmont, a woman's life is in danger. I think that should be all that matters right now."

Lareina felt herself walking slower and slower. She was having more difficulty keeping up with Tony. Her spirit and her body were beyond fatigued. A combination of her injuries; lack of nutrition; dehydration; and lack of rest left her body was crying out for her to stop and take it easy. She knew she couldn't stop, though. Nor could she turn around and go the other way, though she desperately wanted to. If she tried, she knew that Tony would undoubtedly kill her. Lareina sighed heavily and continued on, following Tony's tracks.

Her leg, which he had so deeply sliced with the knife, was beginning to throb. Lareina looked at it and her entire leg had turned red. She simply assumed the electrical tape was bothering her skin. She really wanted to take care of her painful leg, but Tony would not let her have the time to stop and tend to it.

The only sound that either one of them could hear for miles was the crunching of the frozen leaves under their feet.

After countless hours of hiking through the woods, Tony finally stopped. He placed the blanket down. Lareina sighed out of relief. Her body flopped down onto the blanket out of pure exhaustion.

"Let's stop here. We need to eat, at least. We'll have to get going again in a little while, though." Tony said.

Tony sat down on the blanket next to Lareina. Slowly, she pulled herself up and sat up. She opened her purse, and they ate some crackers and some small hard candies. It terribly lacked the nutrition that Lareina so greatly needed, but there had only been so much room in her bag when she packed.

"Tony, may I ask you a question?" Lareina asked quietly.

"Yeah. What's on your mind, love bug?"

"Why the cabin? Why did you bring me there?

"I could understand if you had brought me there because you had seen it once or it meant something to you somehow.

"But with the connection to all of Dominick's problems, why on Earth would you bring me there?"

"I didn't know there was another case against Dominick.

"He had promised me after his release that he was done with that shit. Obviously, he lied to me."

"But why do you both go there? I guess I just don't understand."

Tony sighed and paused for a moment before he spoke. "That cabin belongs to our family. Our grandfather had built it decades ago.

"It was supposed to be a family vacation spot."

"And it wasn't?" Lareina was perplexed by Tony's comment.

"I guess it kind of was. But I mean the whole family would come over: aunts, uncles, cousins. All of us, every time. It was always extremely tight quarters when we'd stay there."

Lareina nodded. "I can imagine that."

"It just wasn't fun being so crowded. There was no privacy. With such a big family, staying in that kind of proximity to each other was not enjoyable for any of us - especially the kids. And then..." Tony's voice trailed off, and he looked away.

"And then what?" Lareina sincerely wondered what memories were being stirred in Tony's mind.

Tony sighed before continuing. "Then, there was Uncle Sal."

"Uncle Sal?"

"Uncle Sal was my father's older brother.

"He'd come with us every time there was a trip up here."

"Ok?"

"Late at night, Uncle Sal would visit all of us kids. The boys and the girls."

Lareina looked at Tony puzzled.

"Uncle Sal would touch us, and make us do horrible things. We all had to do whatever he asked. He would threaten and scare us in order to get us to do stuff. There was no way to escape or be safe from him. We had nowhere to go, and we were afraid to tell because of his threats. No one was ever spared from Uncle Sal's sick pleasures – every fucking kid in the family was molested by that bastard." Tony's bottom lip began to quiver. "Every fucking time we stayed here! There was not one trip where we were ever safe! It was never a God damn vacation! That fucking asshole stole our childhoods!" He screamed out.

"Oh my God! I am so sorry, Tony. I didn't mean to bring anything bad up." Lareina said quietly.

Tony sighed, and then turned to Lareina. "I know you didn't mean to. You didn't know. I never told you that before, so it's ok.

"Anyway, I guess Dominick and I both go back there for our own reasons. Maybe it's to somehow make it our place and erase all the bad memories."

As much as she detested him, Lareina actually felt pity for the pain he had endured as a child. Her heart went out to him. A part of her actually wanted to reach out and comfort him in some way, but she knew she couldn't. If she did, she would only be feeding into his sickness and unpredictable behavior. Though she didn't want to mislead him, she still felt sadness and pity for the little boy Tony once was; the little boy who had been so badly abused.

Another day was rapidly slipping away. It was late afternoon by the time the underwater team had finally arrived. Several men began to set up a small camp with their wet suits, oxygen tanks, a large crane and other equipment. Marc could tell that the set up alone was going to take a while. He feared the length of this process would only endanger Lareina further, but it was his only lead – and only hope. Silently, he prayed that she was still alive.

Just over two more hours had been lost when the men had finally geared up, and started heading into the water. Marc prayed for a sign, a miracle, anything.

The underwater team came in and out of the river several times. Little heads could be seen bobbing around various areas of the river. They swam all throughout the river, trying to find any signs of the Mustang.

The sun was just about gone over the horizon, and there was still no sign of the car. Marc had lost all hope. Suddenly, a small head popped up from the water and began signaling all the other police. Marc ran over to the river bank.

The underwater officer took off his scuba gear so he could speak. "I think I found your car, sir," he said.

"What?! Are you sure?" Marc was flooded with emotion: confusion, excitement, nervousness, and anxiousness all hit him at once.

"Yes sir," the officer in the river said. "There's definitely a car down here, and I think it's the one you've been looking for."

Marc turned around to all the other officers standing around behind him. "Get the crane over here! NOW!"

Very slowly and cautiously, the large machine was brought over to the river bank. Marc couldn't stand the slow pace at which every one else seemed to be moving. He so desperately wanted to get this car, and to finally save Lareina. Once the crane was finally in place, several officers scattered over to it and began hooking up chains, and getting the machine ready. The diver who had spotted the car helped the crane driver to line it all up.

Marc waited impatiently during the process. He tapped his foot with anxiety, and continuously took both hands and grabbed his hair. This was taking too long. The moon was inching its way higher and higher in the sky. Although this was a good sign, it still wasn't bringing Lareina home.

After too much time had been lost setting up, the diver, along with the other divers took the crane hooks and went back under the water.

Several hours after the operation began, the crane slowly started to pull. Inch by slow moving inch, a car began to emerge from out of the cold, dark river waters. Much to Marc's delight a wet, ruined, red 1984 Mustang was dangling from the crane's hooks.

"That's it! We've got him, we've finally got him! It won't be long now before we get this fucker and save Lareina," Marc said to himself. His smile couldn't be brighter than it was at this moment.

Chapter 17

As they continued on their aimless journey through the dark winter night, Lareina felt her leg was increasingly aching and hurting. The pain was considerable. Thinking that it was because she constantly slipping, twisting her ankles and falling on the uneven frozen terrain because of her kitten heels, Lareina nonchalantly slipped them off as they hiked through the forest. She didn't know if they would help lead to her rescue but she hoped it would at least ease the pain in her leg.

Tony wasn't giving her any time to slow down, so hopefully walking barefoot would help her to keep up with his brisk pace. He again hardly gave them enough time to eat, rest, or even relieve themselves. Lareina prayed with each step, though, that she would somehow be found.

"Ok, my turn to ask a person question," Tony said, just a few steps ahead of Lareina.

"Ok?" She skipped a few steps to catch up and walk within listening distance of him.

"Lareina, you told me that you weren't dating when we were in class; and you had never...well, ya know."

Lareina paused for a moment before she understood what Tony was referring to. "Oh! Yes, that's true. So?"

"Well, why not, Lareina?"

"Tony, it's hard to explain. I – it – it just means a lot to me and my family."

"How so? I want to understand."

"Ok. Well, I'm Boricua."

"Huh?"

"I'm Puerto Rican, Tony. Even though my parents have always been legal U. S. citizens, they still had to work very hard – just like immigrants - when they got here.

"My parents, my brother and I all had to learn a new language. We had to learn a new language and adjust to a new culture. My parents came here with so very little. They had to work extremely hard to get everything they had.

"They took on so many jobs just so that my brother and I could have a good education and potential opportunities that simply did not exist in Puerto Rico."

"I don't see what that has to do with you dating."

"It's simple, really. I saw how hard my family sacrificed just for me and I was not going to let that be in vain.

"I wanted to show them how much I appreciated what they had done for us. So, I studied hard and I always worked. It was all for them – for their sacrifice. My first obligation is to my family, not to just any man. The right man would understand; they always told me that and I fully believe it.

"Besides, I was raised to be a good Catholic. My parents instilled morals into my brother and I. Between my family and my beliefs, I was simply living my life the best way I knew how."

"But, why did you always turn me down, Lareina?" The sound of Tony's voice saying her name was grating to Lareina's ears.

"Because like I said, my first obligation was - and always is - to my family, not to any man. They wanted me to have a good life and career, so that was always my top priority."

"But if you would have just gone with me..."

"What? What do you mean?"

"You made me take you. You made me bring you out here. You made me do this.

"If you would have just said yes – if you would have just gone out on one date with me, things could have been so much simpler. We could have just dated normally. We wouldn't have to worry about the police tearing us apart like we do now."

Lareina sighed at Tony's twisted perception. He clearly had no understanding of boundaries or respect. Unsure of how to respond to his comment, Lareina simply replied, "well, things always happen for a reason." It was all she could think of to say. She detested the idea that her personal beliefs had been disrespected and broken simply because she held no romantic interest in Tony at all.

"I guess they do. It doesn't matter, anyway. You're mine now. I own you; that was already established.

"When we consummated our love, you gave me something that you can't give anyone else. That means you're mine."

Lareina dare not say what she really thought. She knew that there was neither consummation of a marriage, nor any love in Tony's evil and selfish act. She refused to be owned by him, or to allow his act change her beliefs or self-perception. She had not been a willing participant. Her love and her body were still hers to give to the right person at the right time. She quietly reminded herself of that constantly to help take away the power from Tony's words and actions.

Lareina continued to walk behind him in silence, despising Tony more and more with each passing moment.

"Where is that tree, Lareina?" Marc whispered to himself. He had been searching the area all around the lake where the car had been found for nearly an entire day. There were no walking paths to be seen, nor any trees with an "x" on them.

Marc knew that Lareina was always precise; he was simply not looking in the right area. As he walked back around, Marc saw an exhausted Chief Wilmont sitting by his car.

"Chief, where is that cabin you were telling me about? The one in the Dominick Covelli case?"

"Not too far from here, Raymer. Go up that way, about a half mile," the Chief pointed behind himself. It was clear that he wasn't moving.

"I want a few uniformed officers to go with me."

The Chief sighed. "Fine. I'll send you up with Learner, Pasternak, and Martinez."

"I should have a few CSI investigators there as well, just in case."

"God damn it, Raymer! How the hell do you not drive your Chief just absolutely insane?!" Chief Wilmont sighed again. "Alright, I'll dispatch a crew to meet you up there."

"Thank you," Marc replied firmly. He then began the arduous task of hiking up towards the cabin, the last light of the day illuminating his path. The uniformed officers weren't too far behind him.

As Marc walked away, he thought he heard the Chief telling one of the uniformed officers that Lareina had to have been murdered by now and that this was all just a wild goose chase. Marc refused to accept the Chief's cynicism as truth. He knew they were close, and he was bound and determined to bring Lareina home alive.

After a decent half mile trek, the trees separated and there before Marc stood the infamous cabin. It was old, dirty and looked abandoned. Marc quickly grabbed a large flash light.

Marc called the uniformed officers over. "Have your weapons drawn and be prepared for anything. We don't know if they're still in there or not."

Stealthfully, the four policemen approached the cabin.

Leading the way, Marc, with his gun drawn, kicked in the front door. There were no obvious signs of life. Marc turned on his flash light. He then signaled for them to all spread out and search the entire dwelling.

The officers did not find any people, and marked the cabin as clear. Then the group began fully examining the cabin. The floor creaked underneath the feet of all the officers.

"Hey, Raymer! Check this out!" Pasternak was in the back room which had once been used as a kitchen. Marc ran back to find a propane tank, a blanket, dishes, and some miscellaneous food stuffs left on the floor. Tony had definitely held her here. Marc figured the visit from the police on Dominick's case had frightened Tony enough that he packed up what he could and went running with Lareina. He couldn't tell how long it had been since they had been in the cabin, but he knew they were definitely on the right track.

"Collect all of that as evidence. Also, have the CSI team check it for finger prints, DNA – the whole nine yards," Marc ordered.

Within moments, a few members of the CSI team then went into the kitchen to take pictures and collect the evidence as Marc had instructed.

Marc continued to walk around the cabin, inspecting every inch of the floor and walls. As he walked around, he found a small door. He opened it. It must have been used as a closet at one time. It was quite narrow, and very dark.

As Marc glanced around the closet with the aid of his flash light, he found a drop of blood on the floor. "I need a CSI here now!"

A CSI investigator ran over to Marc and joined him in the tiny closet.

"Take pictures of that blood stain, get a swab and take it back to your lab for testing. This is important. This is good. It's a really good sign."

"A good sign, sir?"

"It's just one blood drop. It means that Lareina is probably injured, but she is still alive. It's not a significant amount of blood. One drop of blood simply does not equal murder. Based on this, I think it's more than safe to say that she is still alive.

"By the way, I want a rush on that sample. It could be the difference between life and death for this girl."

"Yes Detective Raymer," the CSI investigator then did as she was told.

Marc walked around the main room of the cabin. It was clean – too clean. Marc knew the room should not look this good. The entire building was dilapidated, and yet this room seemed to be in decent shape. Going on his hunch, Marc borrowed a black light from one of the CSI investigators.

Methodically, he looked over every inch of the walls. There was nothing. No signs of life, bleach or other cleaning products. The walls had not been touched.

Marc then scanned the floor. There was evidence of large areas that had been bleached all over the floor. Marc's heart sank. These spots were large and numerous. He feared that they might have been used to clean blood off the floor. Marc's mind now raced with thoughts that Lareina had been murdered by Tony Covelli.

Lareina's leg still hurt severely as they walked the day away. A new morning and afternoon had long come and gone, and yet the pair still had not rested. Lareina still refused to let on that she was in any pain. She feared that Tony would take advantage of it. Lareina looked over the river's horizon. The sun was going down on another day in her captivity.

Lareina followed Tony as best she could through the darkening woods. She struggled immensely on the rugged, cold, and uneven ground. She fought to keep a normal, steady walking pace, but with each step immense pain shot up through her entire leg. Fearing for her life, Lareina battled her affliction silently and followed in Tony's path.

Countless hours of walking had passed when Tony finally took the blanket and laid it out for them.

"We'll eat and get a bit of rest, but we can't stay here long," he said.

"Yes sir."

Another dinner of crackers and river water would have to suffice for nutrition. After a silent meal, Tony laid down on the blanket and pulled Lareina close to him. Lareina lay with her back towards Tony; she sighed, and waited for the sky to become completely black.

Once the stars had been sitting in the sky for a while, Lareina slowly wiggled away from Tony. Lareina was thankful that Tony was a deep sleeper and he did not notice Lareina's absence.

By the light of the moon, she quietly rummaged through her purse and found a receipt, a pencil, and another sanitary pad. On the back of the receipt, she drew an "x" with the coordinates to the cabin. She then marked the path that she and Tony had been walking. She drew circles where she had left her shoes, the pen, and other random items along the way. She continued the line of their path to an approximate location where she and Tony were now. It was a crude and simplistic map at best, but she thought it might just help to guide the police to her.

As quietly as she could, she walked back a few steps. Suddenly, Tony stirred. He grunted and rolled around on the blanket. Lareina stopped, holding her breath so as not to wake him. Her heart raced at the thought of him discovering her. She stood perfectly still, frightened for what may happen next. He grunted again, rolled on to his side, and then there was silence. After a moment of pure stillness, Lareina realized he was still sleeping. Lareina sighed a huge sigh of relief.

She then continued to walk back quietly. She wanted to post her map where the police would find it, but also where Tony wouldn't suspect anything.

Lareina finally felt she was far enough away. She took the napkin and wrapper and used them to stick the map to a tree. She put it just below eye level so that Tony wouldn't notice, should he look back for any reason.

Moving quickly, Lareina made her way back to the blanket and eased her way back down. All she could do was hope all of that her clues were bringing someone closer to saving her.

Marc decided to broaden his search around the cabin. The Mustang sat dripping and water pooled around it on the cold ground of the forest. The water on the car glistened in the early morning sun. The police still waited for confirmation that it truly was Tony's car. Marc figured he could still find more clues while they waited for the confirmation.

Marc looked all around him. All he could see were trees. He was fixated on Lareina's message that "x" marked a specific spot. He was bound and determined to find whatever that "x" might have been.

As he walked around the forest, Marc could not help but be taken in by the size of the trees that surrounded him. They were endlessly tall, magnificently colored; they were awe inspiring. Marc continued to walk through the forest looking for any sign of an "x" - perhaps even two trees that crossed and formed an "x" shape. So far, his search had turned up nothing. He could not find an "x" in any way. He knew there had to be an "x" in the area somewhere and he would continue to search until he found it.

As Marc continued to wander through the forest, he noticed one particularly large, brightly colored and very thick tree. It was significantly larger than the other trees around it. There was something very unique about this tree; it stood out from the others. It would be quite a walk to get to it, but Marc decided that he needed to investigate this large tree.

Marc eventually reached the tree. He put his hand on its large, thick trunk. It was strong and solid. He was inspired by the impressiveness of this one particular tree. He walked all around the wide tree, with his hand still touching its trunk when something slapped him in the eye. Startled, Marc looked up. A piece of fabric had been nailed into the tree and it was waving in the wind. The nailed fabric was on the inside of a large carved "x" on the tree. Marc stared at the carving and fabric. It was the "x"! Lareina had carved that "x" into this tree, and somehow nailed the piece of fabric into this tree in order to gain attention, and help guide them to her. This was the "x" that Lareina's message had been referring to all along. The coordinates, the "x." It all came together.

Marc was more than impressed - he was very proud of her. Lareina showed a strength, intelligence and resourcefulness that he rarely saw in other abducted people. She was indeed a fighter. Seeing the "x" and the fabric, Marc knew without a doubt that she was still alive.

"Good girl," Marc whispered. He stood in awe of her work for minutes. It was quite spectacular to behold. He had no idea how she would have been able to create such a marvelous sign, but she did. Marc was thoroughly impressed.

Marc knew the piece of fabric was going to be crucial in her retrieval. It looked like it had been from a piece of her clothing. Using that fabric, canine units would have a much easier time following her scent and finding her.

Marc still stared at the tree, and took out his police radio. "Fresno PD, anyone on this channel?"

"Wilmont, Chief of police."

"Just the man I was looking for! Wilmont, it's Raymer. You need to come up here now! I found something good – something amazing. And you'll need to dispatch as many canine units as you can. I think - no, I know we're close. Damn close."

Chief Wilmont sighed into the radio. "Raymer, I am really getting sick of your circus. Did you know that your Chief, Karl Hamilton, has already fucking called me three times about you and this damn case just this morning alone?!"

"Good! Now you can call him back and tell him we have a viable lead, and we will be bringing her home within the next twenty four hours or so."

"You just don't get it, do you Raymer? I do not have the time, money or man power to continue to chase down a fucking dead woman!"

"We haven't found a body yet, now have we?"

There was silence before Chief Wilmont finally spoke. "No," he unwillingly agreed.

"Well since there's no body Chief Wilmont, we need to keep searching. Unless and until you can prove to me that she's dead, I want people working this case around the clock.

"Now, get up here. I'm north of the cabin by about a quarter mile. And dispatch those canine units to this same locale, do you understand me?"

No answer. Marc waited. After several moments, the Fresno Chief grunted, indicating that he would comply.

"Honey, get up!" Tony was nudging Lareina. "We slept too long. Dawn has already broken, we really need to go."

Lareina moaned. Her body was so weak, mal-nourished and dehydrated. It took every ounce of her strength just to keep her eyes open.

"I – I can't, Tony," she mumbled.

"I know you're tired, honey. We just have to go a little further. We can't let them find us." Tony pulled her up by the arm. Lareina's body collapsed in his grasp.

"No, Tony..." Lareina's voice faded off.

"We have to go!" There was panic in his voice.

Lareina wearily looked up at him. He could see she was weak and exhausted. He desperately wanted to keep on their expedition east, but he also feared that she could possibly die from exhaustion. Losing her was a risk he didn't want to take. Tony wanted Lareina to be with him for ever. Losing her to exhaustion was simply not an option for him.

Tony sighed. He refused to carry her while hiking through the woods. He wanted her to be able to walk on her own. Tony looked at her for a moment, unsure what to do. Lareina's eyes rolled back, and then she flopped backwards in his arms.

Gently, he placed her back on the blanket. He let her lay there sleeping. He wouldn't - he couldn't let her rest for long, though.

The Fresno Chief was also quite impressed by Lareina's handiwork. He and Marc waited for the canine units by the large carved tree.

"You gotta give that girl some serious credit. Not many people would think or even be able to do something like this," Chief Wilmont said.

"Indeed. She's a smart girl. She's irrefutably a fighter, too.

"Once we get the canines on her smell from this, we'll finally have her safe and away from this asshole. We're so close to getting her home safely."

"Let's hope so. I do think you have a good point, Raymer; but we still can't be sure he hasn't done anything to her out there. I just really hope you're right on this one. But if she can do this, I can't imagine she'd give up without a fight."

"I thought you had completely given up on her, Chief."

"I had. But, you're right, Raymer. I'm man enough to admit when I was wrong. If she can do this, then she is probably still alive around here somewhere."

"Now you understand why I've been so obsessed with this case, Chief." Marc said.

"Yeah," Chief Wilmont softly replied.

The canine units arrived a few minutes later. Five officers each with their own canine companion stood in a row. Chief Wilmont then called all the involved police over to the tree.

"Ok, guys. Listen up! This material has the scent of missing person Lareina Oliveira. We need you to use this material - and her scent - to help lead us in her direction." Chief Wilmont said.

Marc spoke up next. "Remember everyone, she has been abducted and is still with her kidnapper. As far as we know, they are on foot. More than likely they haven't gotten too far without a map and sufficient food supplies.

"Anthony Covelli, the abductor, is considered to be armed and dangerous. We need to use all precautionary tactics when approaching him.

"We do not know the physical condition of Lareina Oliveira. If she is still alive, and we do have full reason to believe so, we need to get her medical treatment as quickly as possible.

"I know this has not been an easy case on any one. I greatly appreciate the help and cooperation of all you from the Fresno PD.

"We've got 'em, boys. We are right behind them. Let's go find them and bring and end to this case!" Marc said to the group.

One canine officer pulled down the fabric and all the dogs began to sniff it. Within just seconds, the dogs began pulling and racing to the East.

"I guess we're headed to the east," Marc said to Chief Wilmont.

The group of police officers all started walking and running east, hoping they could get to Lareina in time.

Lareina and Tony walked slowly in broad daylight. They had gotten a much later start than Tony had wanted, and Lareina was still visibly weak and tired. Tony was worried that he could be losing her. He wanted to get her help, but knew that he couldn't get her the medical attention she needed right now.

Lareina's leg was obviously red, and she sporadically limped on it, though she said nothing. She knew that Tony could see her fatigue, but she still insisted on putting on a facade that she was physically able to carry on. So, she silently followed Tony. With each step, she hoped that her ordeal would soon be over.

They had been walking for most of the day when Lareina thought she could hear dogs in the distance. She assumed her weary state was causing her to hear things. She continued to limp in silence.

Tony stopped walking just a few moments later. "Did you hear that?"

Dogs could in fact be heard. It wasn't just her imagination, Tony heard them too! They could also hear various voices shouting, though they could not make out what was being called out. The voices and dog barks sounded as if they were getting closer; but they still sounded to be an infinity away to Lareina.

Lareina looked up at Tony puzzled. Could it be that she would finally be rescued?

"Did you do this?" Tony angrily grabbed her by the arms.

"What? No, Tony. I did nothing. How could I have gotten anyone here? You threw away my cell phone days ago, remember? It's just been us, Tony. There's no way I could have contacted anyone.

"Unless – Do you think Dominick would have said something? Is it possible that after the investigation with that little girl he said something to work out a deal?"

"Ya know, that is a possibility. I never thought of that, but my asshole of a brother would do anything to save his own ass. Fucker!"

Tony rapidly wrapped Lareina's hair around his wrist and began dragging her behind him. She soon fell down and Tony started to fall backwards from her weight. Quickly, he yanked her back up with all his might and he started to drag her again.

"Tony, please! Stop! I'll walk as fast as I can!" Lareina begged him.

"No." He stopped, let go and dropped her to the ground. She fell face first onto the dirt, rocks and leaves. Lareina spat out a leaf.

Unbreakable Hostage

Dazed and beaten, she hesitantly looked up at her captor.

He looked down at her. There was anger and rage in his eyes.

"Tony, what's going on?"

"If I can't have you, no one can! You're mine! They won't take you from me! I won't let them!"

Tony pulled Lareina up by the back of her shirt. He dragged her along the ground until they got to the river bank.

With hardly any effort, Tony threw Lareina into the river face down. His fat hand pressed down upon her shoulders to keep her in place. Lareina felt him using a tremendous amount of strength to hold her down. Her arms and legs flailed around, but it was of no help. Her breath was escaping her quickly. She fought and twisted her head from side to side trying to suck in any air that she could, but all she took in was water. Seeing her struggle, Tony pushed her down even harder. Lareina's arms continued to splash around. She desperately tried to hit Tony, but she was defenseless against him. With her air supply almost completely gone, Lareina's arms began to flap less and less. Slowly, her struggle decreased until she finally stopped moving all together.

Tony continued to hold her down for a few more seconds. It took some time before the reality of what he was doing set in. Seeing her motionless body frightened him. With as much thrust as he used to force her down, he pulled her back up and onto the bank of the river.

Tony pressed on Lareina's chest a few times. Finally, her eyes opened and she spat up a large amount of water and began coughing and gasping for air.

Tony looked down on Lareina, and she saw an odd, frightening tenderness in his eyes. "You're safe with me, sweetie. No one will ever hurt you, I promise," he whispered.

Chapter 18

The search team continued to follow the dogs' lead as the day slipped into night. With various flashlights flashing around the forest, the hunt for Lareina and Tony diligently continued.

The team took occasional breaks to rest, eat, and to allow the dogs the same. The team never rested for long, though. They knew they were too close to saving Lareina; they didn't want to lose any more time than was absolutely necessary.

As the army of police picked up again and continued in their progression, one officer shouted out, "halt," and his voice echoed through the forest.

The troops stopped and went over to his waving flashlight. There was a pen on the ground. The group circled around him to see.

At first, it almost seemed insignificant. It was simply a pen. It could have come from anyone at any time.

"Do you think this means anything?" One canine officer asked.

"It could be nothing, but it could also mean that she's alive," Marc snapped back. "We have to consider every little detail. Nothing can be ruled out or dismissed. This might be another attempt from her to lead us to them."

The pen was treated as evidence and placed in a bag, and then the group continued on their night search.

Lareina's leg continued to throb and felt swollen. The pain was becoming unbearable.

As Tony slept deeply on the cold, hard ground, Lareina quietly stepped away from him. With great apprehension she ripped the electrical tape off the wound on her leg.

The sting of the tape ripping her skin was nothing compared to the pain of the cold night air assaulting her gash. Biting her lip from the pain, she balled up the tape and threw it as far as she could. She hoped that it would be yet another lead for the police to help bring her to safety.

Lareina gently placed her hand around the wound. Cautiously, she pressed and touched her leg. It felt hot and distended. There was no question in her mind: she was battling a deep infection in her leg. "Damn it," Lareina whispered to herself.

As quietly as she could, she stepped into the cold river water with much trepidation. As soon as she stepped into the river the water burned and stung her injury. Lareina bit her lip hard and fought to remain silent. The pain was agonizing. She began to focus on taking in deep breaths so she could restrain herself from screaming in anguish.

Lareina knew that she needed to clean out this wound as best she could, yet she had to stay quiet so that she wouldn't wake Tony. Gently she swished her leg in the water, and she gently massaged her wound under the water. Tears of pain raced down Lareina's face while she allowed the cold river water to get inside her wound and clean her leg.

Lareina swiftly washed her leg, and then she limped back up to where Tony lay. Slowly, painfully she eased her way down to lie on the blanket next to him in the cold, black night. The tears continued to roll down her cheeks. Between the pain, the fatigue, and her desperation to get home, she could no longer hold the tears back. She prayed that this night: the darkest of nights, would be the last of this horrific and horrendous terrorization.

The night wore on, and yet another halt had been called out. The group gathered to see a pair of small women's shoes.

172

Marc picked them up and examined them. The heels were nearly completely worn off. It took him a moment to realize that Lareina had used her shoes to carve that tree. She left them in the woods as a sign of her trail path with Tony.

"Oh my God," Marc whispered. He stopped to take a deep breath. "Bag these as evidence. We're very close now. We need to move quickly."

As day broke, the search continued. The policemen and dogs were exhausted but they knew they were too close to give up on Lareina now. As they continued to follow the track lead by the dogs, another officer called out for a halt.

"Look at this," the young officer said pointing to a crude map stuck to a tree by sanitary pad.

Marc grabbed it. On the map was an "x," with the coordinates from that once mystifying text message. It was the location of the cabin. Lareina had marked their path to that point as well as their general direction; and she had circled where she had left the pen and her shoes.

"Ok, listen up!" Marc called out. "We're getting close – extremely close. I know we're all tired, but we've got to be ready for anything. With a clue like this, we could be apprehending them in just a matter of a few hours. I need all of you to hang in there and stay sharp.

"Let's keep going!"

The small army of police went back onto the trail following this new map, hoping they could save the young woman before it was too late.

Tony woke Lareina just as the sun began to rise over the horizon. "Honey, get up. We need to get moving." Tony rolled up the blanket and picked it up. Lareina lay still for a second, she was still very groggy when he suddenly took her hand and led her deeper into the woods.

173

"We should go into the river, in case they still have the dogs on us. This way we'll fool them – they won't be able to track us if there's no scent. And then we'll be safe from them," he said. He grabbed her hand and began walking down towards the river. Lareina disgustedly followed Tony's lead, and once again found herself in the biting cold water of the Merced River.

They trudged through the water as best they could. The cold river water was resistance enough, but the rocky bottom had Tony and Lareina slipping frequently in their journey. They were slow moving, but they were still moving nonetheless.

The water continued to bite and sting at Lareina's leg, but she dared not let on that she was suffering any pain.

As much as she was nauseated by him and desperately wanted to let go of Tony's hand, Lareina knew that if she did it would certainly mean her death. With great hesitancy, she followed him along on the cold, rocky, uneven river floor.

The day passed slowly as Tony and Lareina continued to slosh through the river. There was no sign of the police any more. Neither Tony nor Lareina saw anyone or heard anything. The forest was eerily silent except for the movement of the water from the pair's walk; and they continued on that walk without saying a word to each other. Lareina wondered if they had indeed lost the team of police, or if the search had possibly even been called off.

The cold finally got the better of Lareina, and she began to shiver. Her teeth chattered, though she desperately tried to control it. She feared what may happen if Tony knew she was cold and weak. Despite her best efforts her teeth clacked loudly.

"You're cold?" Tony asked.

Lareina simply nodded her head.

Tony pulled Lareina through the water, and they finally sat on the bank of the river. Tony wrapped the blanket around Lareina as she shivered. "It's ok, honey. They won't get us. I won't let them hurt you."

Lareina said nothing, looking at the ground beneath her.

Tony went through her purse and pulled out a small bag of crackers. "Here, eat this, baby," he said extending his hand.

Lareina weakly took the crackers, and quietly nibbled on the dry snack.

They sat in silence as the sun inched its way through the sky.

"We're going to have to move again soon," Tony finally said.

Lareina did not mutter a word to her captor.

"Unless..." Tony looked at Lareina.

Slowly, she turned and looked back at him. There was an angry, evil hunger and fierceness in his eyes that she recognized. Not again, she prayed. She hoped that her fears were unfounded. Tony moved in closer, though, making her comprehend what evil thoughts swirled in his mind.

"No," Lareina's voice was so weak, it was nearly inaudible.

"If they find us together, they'll see there's nothing wrong."

"No," Lareina repeated herself, but with a bit more strength in her voice.

"It's ok, honey. This is for the best. I won't hurt you."

Lareina's eyes grew large and wide with fear. "No," she whispered a third time.

"It's ok," Tony tried to reassure her.

Lareina slowly began to slip away backwards and distance herself from him.

"It's ok," Tony said again as he followed Lareina.

Suddenly, dogs could be heard barking in the distance. Lareina prayed they would find her in time.

"Damn it! They're getting close!

"Come on, honey. We have to," Tony said as he pulled the blanket off the cold, wet woman.

Once more, Larcina backed up. Her hand slipped on a wet rock, and she fell onto her back. The pain of falling backwards sent a horrific shock through her spine. Knowing what evil intentions crept around Tony's mind, Lareina quickly picked herself back up again and continued to crawl backwards.

Tony crawled forward, lurking closer and closer to Lareina.

"No," Lareina began to cry. "Please, Tony, don't!"

"This is for the best – for us!"

Tony leaped on top of Lareina. He began unbuttoning her shirt.

"No!" Lareina screamed with what little strength she had.

The dogs heard in the background were getting closer. Lareina prayed they would reach her quickly.

Tony ripped Lareina's shirt off completely. He began to struggle with her bra. Lareina tried to fight him off, but Tony was far too strong.

She weakly kicked him and was able to push him off of her. She slid on the cold, wet ground as she tried to get away.

Tony came running at her and tackled her, pinning her down.

"No, no!" Lareina cried. Her voice was strained, but it still echoed through the trees. All she could do was hope that her voice was leading the police directly to her.

Tony unzipped his pants and began to undo Lareina's pants. Lareina pulled her knees up to her body. Tony grabbed her ankles with great strength, and pulled her legs down. Lareina no longer had the strength to fight back. She lay there half way undressed, crying.

"Tony, no! Please, don't!" Lareina's voice was quiet and weak.

Tony forced himself on top of her, and forced his way into her body. Unknowingly, Lareina loudly cried out in pain.

Knowing that she couldn't just lay there but that she needed to fight to survive, Lareina used ever ounce of strength she had and punched Tony in the eye. She was amazed as she watched Tony flop off of her. Quickly, she pulled her pants back up.

Tony rose, his face was red with pure anger.

Lareina stood up as swiftly as she could and began running in the direction of the dogs they heard earlier.

Tony gave chase, his fat body struggling to keep up with Lareina's surprisingly fast pace.

"Help me! I'm here!" Lareina called out, hoping the police would follow the echo of her voice.

She turned behind her to see Tony was losing his stride. She continued to push herself and ran as fast as her weakened body would let her.

The dogs became more and more excitable as the police continued on the trail, just a short distance behind Tony and Lareina. Every officer walked a quick pace or even ran to keep up. They knew they would be rescuing her soon.

"Halt!" Another officer could be heard crying out.

The group stopped and ran over to see. A small balled up piece of electrical tape had been found.

Marc picked it up. One of the dogs began lunging towards him and barking. Lareina's scent was on that tape. Marc could only imagine what it had been used for.

Along with the pen, shoes and map, the electrical tape was gathered for evidence.

Just as the group of police were about to continue on, they could hear a woman's voice calling in the distance. It sounded as if she was calling out for help. There was an ominous silence among the police as they heard the woman's cries.

"That could be her," Marc told the group. "We have to split up. I want half the group to continue to follow the dogs. I will lead the other group in the direction of her voice. I'm sure we'll meet up. Let's go!"

It sounded as if Lareina was getting closer to the barking dogs. She continued to run in that direction, hoping she would quickly find safety. As she ran she began to feel weak and depleted of all energy. Her numerous injuries were getting wearing her down. She knew she couldn't stop now, though. She was too close to being rescued.

Suddenly, she was pushed forward from behind and she fell face first to the ground. Tony had managed to catch up to her and now his heavy body lay on her. Lareina fought to breathe under his weight. She took in as much air as she could. She refused to let him win now.

She reached out and tried to crawl forward from underneath him. She was able to move forward just a few inches.

Tony reached out and pinned her arms down.

"Help!" Lareina weakly cried out. Because of Tony's weight on top of her, her cry sounded more like a squeak. Tony reveled in the fact that there was no way the police could have heard her.

"I'm here, honey. They won't hurt you. You're just confused right now," Tony whispered.

Lareina twisted and wiggled her way under Tony. She was able to roll onto her back, and she stared at Tony's round, sweaty, dirty face. With an incredible intensity in her eyes she said, "I'm not confused."

She noticed that as she moved Tony moved with her. Hoping she could use that to her advantage, Lareina continued to roll back and forth. Tony's thick body was moving with hers. She continued to move and wiggle, still hoping he'd eventually lose his grip and roll off her.

Lareina realized as she was struggling, that her legs were free. Then, Lareina started kicking Tony in his legs and sides with both of her legs. She kicked him several times with great force until he finally let go of her. Lareina scrambled to get up. Just as she began to run again, her weak little ankle twisted, and she fell back to the ground. She turned to see Tony charging up behind her like an angry bull.

"Freeze!" An unrecognized, strong male voice called out.

Tony stopped dead in his tracks.

Lareina looked up towards the direction of the voice. She could not believe the sight before her. They were surrounded by countless uniformed and well dressed police officers, all aiming their guns at Tony.

They had finally come for her! Lareina was safe now; she realized that she would be going home alive. The thought of being rescued consumed her. Although she lay unmoving, Lareina began sobbing uncontrollably.

"No, wait! Can't you see?! We love each other! This is how it has to be!" Tony shouted back to the policeman.

"Anthony, let her go," the policeman said. His voice was strong and intense. He had a distinguishable British accent.

"No! She's mine!" Tony reached forward, grabbed her arm tightly and pulled her in front of him. "You wouldn't hurt a woman, would you?"

"Tony, I'll ask you one more time. Let her go." The British man was stern and unwavering.

"No!" Tony screamed. He wrapped one hand around her neck and began to squeeze.Air began escaping her lungs rapidly. "If you shoot me, you'll also shoot her. You wouldn't want that, now would you?"

"Tony, let Lareina go! She's done nothing to you," the British man tried to reason with Tony.

"If I can't have her, no one can!" His hand squeezed even tighter around her neck. Lareina tried to pry his fat hand off of her, but his grip was too firm.

Tony moved backwards inch by tiny inch, Lareina was still fighting to breathe. He wrapped her hair tightly around his other wrist and began to run away, dragging Lareina with him.

Suddenly, Tony lost his grip of her hair. Her head flung forward as a large chunk of hair fell out. Tony quickly tightened his grip around her neck. Lareina was beginning to lose consciousness.

As Lareina slumped forward, there was a loud, deafening pop. Tony fell backwards, losing his control over Lareina. She fell forward landing onto her hands and knees, gasping and choking to breathe.

"Shit!" Tony cried out, his cries of pain echoing through the trees. The British man had shot him in the arm. Tony writhed in pain on the ground, rolling around like a turtle on its shell.

A uniformed officer, along with Marc ran over and pulled Tony up. As they did so, Tony elbowed the uniformed officer in his abdomen. He used such force that the policeman fell back a few steps from Tony and began coughing for air.

Tony then reached out and grabbed Marc's hand. The two struggled for control of Marc's gun. The gun waved dangerously back and forth in the air as the two men fought endlessly for control of the weapon. With the gun moving perilously close to both of their heads, Marc eventually took a step back still gripping the gun tightly.

Tony decided to use the distance between them to his advantage. Tony's short stature gave him an advantage that Marc had not considered. With all of his might, he head-butted Marc right in the middle of his abdomen. Marc lost his grip on the gun as he fell backwards a few steps from the blow.

Without even taking a moment to realizing the severity of his disadvantage, Marc quickly gathered himself up and charged Tony. He pushed him down to the ground with all of his might. The other police officers watched, unable to help since none of them could get a clear target on Tony. The two wrestled and rolled around back and forth fighting for control and dominance. Though Marc was far more muscular than his opponent, they seemed fairly equal in strength as they continued to wrestle for control of the gun, and of the situation. They both grunted through their clenched teeth as they rolled around; each man breathing heavily in the other man's face. It was tremendously intense for the two men, as well as for the officers watching them.

The two continued to wrestle around in the leaves and cold dirt for several minutes. Marc finally seemed to have the advantage and he pulled mightily on the gun to get it out of Tony's fat grasp. Now holding the gun, Marc began to pull his arm forward to hold the gun in Tony's face. Determined not to lose to this British cop, Tony used his weight and pushed Marc down. Tony eventually rolled on top of him. Tony then allowed all of his body weight to flop down on top of Marc. With all his might and weight, Tony sat on Marc in order to incapacitate him.

Marc began gasping for air under Tony's heavy weight. Marc fought valiantly to push Tony off of him, but as the air escaped his lungs he was simply unable to fight back. Seeing that his muscular and formidable opponent was weakening, Tony grabbed Marc. He stood up and pulled up Marc by the arm. Tony hoisted Marc up, while still holding the gun. Tony then twisted Marc around, held Marc in front of himself and held the gun to Marc's head.

"Nobody move!" Tony screamed. "If anyone so much as takes a breath, I will blow his head off." Tony cocked the gun, just to prove that he would have no remorse in shooting Marc.

All of the other officers silently stood in place, guns still aimed at Tony.

Lareina was still on her hands and knees, panting for air. She looked up and saw what was going on. The handsome British policeman was in danger. Lareina knew what Tony was capable of. She couldn't let her rescuer be hurt. Still heaving for air, she looked all around her for a rock. Just out of reach sat a large, round rock. Lareina tried to move quietly so Tony wouldn't be aware of her movements. Cautiously, she reached out and pulled the rock to her.

She continued to stay down. Her body was still dying for air: she knew she'd have to move slowly. She struggled to pick up the rock. It was rather sizable and very heavy for her in her weakened state. She sat for a few moments getting used to the weight of the rock. She struggled for a bit, but she finally stood up. One of the officers looked at her. Lareina stared back and nodded her head. The police officer casually turned his attention back to Tony.

Lareina made her way towards Tony with great trepidation. She was silently moving closer to the malevolent man. She had gotten pretty close to Tony, when a leaf crunched under her small bare foot. Tony whipped around. Lareina quickly pulled her hands behind her back, so Tony wouldn't see the rock.

"Tony, let him go. I'm here – surrendering to you. But only if you will let him go," Lareina said without missing a beat.

"Why are your hands behind your back?"

"To show you that I am fully submitting to you. All I ask is that you let that man go."

"Let him go?! Are you kidding? He fucking shot me!"

"I know. I understand that. But, I can take care of you. You can heal from that wound. Please, Tony. You don't want him. All this time all you've wanted is me, and now I am here surrendering to you."

Marc looked at Lareina with his deep brown eyes. It was as if he could see her thoughts in her hazel eyes. He dared not move or say a word. He was impressed that she was still so sharp after all she had endured physically and mentally.

Lareina slowly stepped to the side and behind Tony. "I'll just wait here until you let him go, ok?" Though Tony seemed to accept Lareina's offer, she could still sense great danger for the Englishman.

Tony looked forward again at all the other police surrounding him. "Ok, you all heard her. She's coming with me. If I let him go, you all have to leave us both alone. Is that understood?"

The police all nodded, each man hoped Tony would not see through the facade.

As Tony spoke, Lareina pulled her arm back as far as she could, as if she was about to throw a baseball. With every last bit of strength and energy in her weary body, she threw the rock forward in the hopes that it would save the British officer. The rock flew through the cold winter air. It seemed surreal to everyone watching. As if in slow motion, the rock made its way through the trees and eventually hit Tony right in the middle of his back.

The rock hit him with such force that it pushed Tony forward. Tony screamed out in pain, pushing Marc out of his grip; the gun was flung forward as the rock hit him. Tony started to fall forward towards the ground. Marc reached up and grabbed his gun from the air. He turned around and shot Tony again, this time in the shoulder. Tony now fell backwards to the ground, screaming and squirming in pain.

Several officers ran over to Tony, pulled him up and handcuffed him. Still screaming at the top of his lungs, Tony was hurriedly dragged away towards all the police vehicles.

Lareina collapsed onto the ground in sheer fatigue. After a few moments, she realized her nakedness in front of the British officer; she pulled her knees to her chest, and tried to cover her small, beaten body.

"Here," the Englishman said, throwing a jacket to Lareina.

She wrapped herself in the jacket, zipping it all the way up so that she was as covered up as possible.

The English man walked towards her. Lareina shivered in fright.

"It's ok," his voice was soft, gentle and caring. "You're safe now. My name is Detective Marcus Raymer. You can call me Marc."

Lareina's wet, glossy eyes blankly looked back at Marc.

He slowly extended his hand to her. Nervously, she reached out and grabbed his hand. With a gentle strength, Marc pulled her up.

Emotion overwhelmed Lareina. She began to sob uncontrollably. Marc lightly wrapped his arms around her and comforted the young woman. They stood in place while Lareina sobbed for several minutes.

After a tender but much needed embrace, Marc slowly led Lareina back to the car.

It was a long, silent walk back to all the police vehicles. Lareina watched as the one patrol car containing Tony drove away. She watched Tony's face through the car window as it disappeared into the trees.

It was a surreal experience. Her ordeal was finally over. She had gotten away from Tony at long last. She was amazed that she was somehow still alive. Lareina tried to absorb every detail of this very moment, realizing that she was truly free.

"Your parents and Sandy will be waiting for you at the hospital in L. A.," Marc softly said to Lareina as they approached his car. Marc reached forward and opened the passenger door of his car for her.

Slowly, with great pain and fear, Lareina eased her way into the passenger seat of Marc's car. Once she seemed to be sitting comfortably, Marc gently closed the car door. Lareina pulled down the visor, and looked in the tiny mirror. She stared deeply into her reflection.

The face looking back at her was not her own. Her lips were swollen and split. Both of her eyes were badly bruised and swollen. Her once bright, stunning hazel eyes were now hidden by the bruises. There were cuts, bruises, abrasions, and swelling all over her face. Her hair was disheveled with pieces of leaves, pebbles and twigs entangled in it. The chunk of hair that Tony had ripped out earlier left a noticeable bald spot. She was no longer the little Hispanic beauty everyone found her to be. Now she looked ugly and deformed. The sight before her was frightening.

For the first time, Lareina looked down at her hands as well. The skin on her wrists was red and raw from the electrical tape. Ugly scars were beginning to form over the cuts he had inflicted upon her wrists. There were countless injuries on her delicate little hands. They were swollen and so badly bruised that they looked almost completely black. Thick black dirt was shoved deeply under her finger nails. Both of her hands were stuck in a claw-like position, no matter how hard she tried to open them.

The reality and severity of her trauma finally struck Lareina. One small tear made its way down Lareina's refined but mangled face.

"You're safe now, Lareina," Marc quietly said. He gently wrapped his large, warm hand around hers. "We're going to bring you back to Los Angeles, and get you medical treatment and food. But we will also need to take your statement.

"As I said, your family and Sandy are waiting for you. You won't be alone. They will be with you through everything, alright? They'll take care of you; they'll stay with you in the hospital. No one will hurt you any more, I promise." His tone was calm and sincere.

Lareina looked up at Marc with a beauty, an innocence, and a helplessness in her eyes that he had never seen before in anyone. He could see how great her fear continued to be. He desperately wanted to take all that pain and fear away for her. Gently, he rubbed her hand with his large, warm thumb to reassure her.

They drove the five hour trek back down to Los Angeles in complete silence: Marc unsure how to comfort his travel companion, and Lareina unable to speak.

Marc continued to kindly caress Lareina's diminutive, damaged hand throughout the five hour drive back home.

Chapter 19

"Hi, Lareina. My name is Anne. I'm from the crime scene investigations unit. I'm here to collect some samples and all the medical information regarding your kidnapping and assaults, ok?

"Some of this will be ok, some of it may hurt; a lot of it may be very emotional for you, but that's ok. I'm not going to hurt you. We'll move at a pace you're comfortable with and do this in the least traumatic way possible, ok?"

Lareina looked at the CSI investigator with tremendous fear in her eyes.

"It's ok. I know this is scary and awkward, but I promise that I'm not going to hurt you. We just need to take pictures and collect some evidence; ok, Lareina?"

Lareina nodded her head. Anne closed the curtain around them, separating Lareina from her family, and the rest of the outside world.

Anne took pictures of Lareina's face, hands, back, and legs: all of her bruises, cuts, and wounds. She scraped some of the dirt from under Lareina's fingernails. She moved slowly, and talked Lareina through every step of the process. Though Lareina was scared and embarrassed, Anne brought her some comfort and reassurance during the lengthy procedure.

A doctor and nurse came in a little while later. The nurse gently took a vaginal sample from Lareina for a rape kit. Afterwards, the doctor performed a pelvic exam. Anne stood by, watching and documenting everything.

It took hours to document every wound; x-ray every broken bone; and clean and treat Lareina's infected leg wound. The horrific ordeal was eventually over.

Lareina tried to remain stoic during all of the testing, poking and prodding. There were times when her emotions got the best of her, and a tear or two would silently escape.

"Ok, Lareina. We're finally done. Thank you so much for your cooperation and for being so brave. What we've done here today will greatly help your case against your assailant," Anne said after all the testing and documentation had been completed.

"Thank you," Lareina weakly replied.

"We'll be in touch," Anne said, placing her hand gently over Lareina's. She then left the hospital room.

After Anne left, Lareina's parents and brother sat with her.

"Oh, mija!" Consuelo cried.

"We're so glad to have you back," Jose said.

"I just can't believe any of it, Papa. It was like a bad dream. You never think something like this will ever happen to you. I was just going to school for my doctorate, not getting myself involved with anything bad or weird.

"I just can't understand why he picked me," Lareina said.

Lareina lay in her hospital bed with multiple IV lines; an oxygen cannula sat in her nose; EKG leads continuously monitored her heart; a drain sat in her infected leg wound; staples closed the wound on her arm; a soft wrap went around her torso several times due to some rib fractures she suffered, and both of her hands were in small casts.

"Well, that bad dream - all of it - is over now, sis," Juanito said. "You're safe; your family is here."

"We'll stay down here as long as you need," Jose said.

"Thank you, Papa."

"For now, though, you should rest," her father lovingly suggested.

"But - wait, Papa! I want to know – I need to know – what happened to Tony?"

"Why the hell do you care about that scumbag, Lareina?" Juanito asked with an angry tone.

"Well, did they take care of his gunshot wounds, or did they bring him directly to jail? I can't rest if I know he's in another hospital. Or worse: here! I want to know he's locked away and can't get out. I want to know I'm safe again. Please tell me he's not here!"

"He's not here, Lareina." Jose said calmly. "That Detective told us he's in a lock down facility at some other hospital until he's well enough to go to prison."

Lareina looked at her father with great concern and fear on her face.

"He's locked away, Lareina. He won't hurt you – he can't hurt you. There are police and security guards all around him. You're safe here, I promise you." Jose reassured his daughter. "Now rest, mija. We want you to get better."

"Yes, Papa," Lareina muttered. She tried to find a comfortable position and closed her eyes, surrendering to her exhaustion.

Juanito stood by the window, the late afternoon sun shining on him. He was alone with his sister. He relished moments like this, for the two siblings rarely got to spend time alone together.

"You doing alright, Sis?"

"Yeah," Lareina sighed.

"Hmmm, that doesn't sound too convincing. What's up?"

"It's going to sound weird, Juanito."

"No, it won't. You've been through a lot, Lareina."

"You're my big sister; you know I worry about you."

"It's just – I keep hearing the music he played in the car when he first took me. It was so scary and haunting. I hear it constantly in my head – even in my nightmares. I can't escape from it at all!"

189

"So, tell me about it." Juanito sat down in a chair next to Lareina, and held her hand as she spoke.

"It was loud, scary heavy metal, Juanito. It just chilled me to the bones hearing it in the car, and it was repeating in my head all day every day while we were out there. I still hear it now! I feel like I'm haunted by a ghost. It was so scary and creepy."

"Well, what did they say in the songs?"

"There was little that I could understand. It was German, Tony said.

"Juanito, he told me about a song of theirs where a woman is chained to a piano and that's how she dies because her kidnapper just makes her play it day and night and he doesn't take care of her.

"Tony took that as inspiration. That's when he taped me to the rocking chair. That's how he broke both my hands." Lareina could no longer fight back the tears. She cried from the depths of her soul.

"It's ok, Lareina," Juanito rubbed his sister's shoulder. "I know it was scary. But you're safe now. You don't have to listen to that music, not any more. Never again, I promise.

"The scariest thing is, Juanito, a part of me actually wants to know what they said."

"Lareina, I know that you have so many questions; so many fears; so many haunting memories. But to focus so intensely on the music will take away from your real healing.

"What does it matter, what they said?"

"I don't know. I guess, in a way – I know it sounds silly, but in a way, I feel as if they were singing about me."

"Well, maybe they were. Maybe they were singing a song of a brave woman who is captured and tortured, but she survives and gets revenge by throwing a rock at her kidnapper's back at the time of her rescue.

"Would that make you feel better?"

"You know," Lareina chuckled through her tears. "I think it would."

"Then that's what they were singing about, ok?"

The two siblings smiled at each other. Lareina seemed relieved at Juanito's idea of a song being sung about her bravery.

"But, Juanito," Lareina started. "How do I get that music out of my head? How will I ever make it stop?"

"Make it the song we just talked about. It's about you, and how strong and brave you are. How you fought back against an evil man and won. Try to make it something positive instead of something so scary, sis."

"I'm sorry you're so haunted by it. I wish I could take it away for you."

"Me too. But I will try what you said," Lareina weakly smiled at her brother.

The sunlight was nearly gone by now.

"I think you need some rest, Lareina. You've been through so much and your body has so much healing to do. I'll let you have some peace, ok?"

"Ok, Juanito. Thank you. I love you."

"I love you too, sis."

Sandy and Lareina's family sat with her in the small hospital room. They talked and laughed loudly. Day by day, Lareina's condition improved; they all relished the beautiful moments they now shared together.

Lareina was much brighter. She was healing well, and she was beginning to feel safe.She was delighted to be surrounded by the people she loved.

A young man came into the hospital room with a bouquet of flowers. Lareina was running out of room for all the flowers and gifts she had received. This was a small bouquet with daisies, baby's breath, and tulips.

"Who is that from?" Lareina asked.

"It says 'Get well soon, Lareina. From Dr. Bauer.'" The young man said.

"That is so sweet!" Lareina was honored that her professor thought of her.

"You had a great professor," Sandy said. "She really helped the police in finding you. They told me that she was quite instrumental in bringing you home."

"I will definitely need to thank her when I get back to school."

"When are you returning to the university, Lareina?" Juanito asked.

"Not for a while. I need to get better first. Plus, I really want my life to feel regular again before I take on such a daunting schedule with classes and all. I don't want any added stresses. I just want to be able to fully focus on my school work, and right now I am simply not able to. When I'm over some of these stresses and fears, I will go back and finish school."

"Good idea mija," Consuelo said.

"It's getting late, Lareina. I hate to leave you, but I need to get back to the house," Sandy said. "I have tests to grade tonight, I'm so sorry."

"It's fine, Sandy. I'm ok."

"Will you be ok if we all leave?" Jose asked.

"Papa, you ask me that question every night. And every night I tell you, I'll be fine. No te preocupes."

"Alright, Lareina. You know I need to watch out for my little girl," Jose said.

"Yes, Papa. I know." Lareina smiled at her father and the rest of her family.

The family all gingerly hugged their dearest Lareina and left her hospital room. Jose turned off the light as he exited.

Lareina tried to get comfortable despite her tubes, wires and bandages. Once she settled in, she closed her eyes.

She had just begun to drift off to sleep when there was a gentle knock at the door. It was towards the end of visiting hours, so Lareina couldn't imagine who would be stopping over at this time of day.

"Lareina?" The voice was warm and familiar. The British accent was a give away: it was Marc.

"Yes. Come in, Detective."

Marc walked into the dim room. The light from the sunset pooled in the room, giving the room an almost brownish hue and everything appeared shadowy.

"Hi," Marc said sheepishly as he came near to her bed. He held a large arrangement of sunflowers. He smiled at the beautiful woman resting in the hospital bed.

"Hi, Detective! It's so good to see you again. What can I do for you?"

"I just wanted to bring you these."

"Oh thank you so much! They're gorgeous! I love sunflowers: they're my favorite! How did you know?"

"I asked your mother," Marc answered as he placed the flowers down on the only open area he could find on the counter.

Lareina smiled brightly at him. "Thank you so much. That was very kind of you. I greatly appreciate it."

"You're quite welcome," he smiled back. "So, how are you doing?"

"I'm ok. You know, I do have some pain and all.

"The worst is the infection in my leg. They have me on IV antibiotics, and once I get home I'll still have to take antibiotics for another month."

"Oh wow! I am so sorry to hear that, Lareina.

"Is there...uhhhh...anything I can do to help?"

"Get me a new leg?" Lareina laughed. It was the first time Marc had heard Lareina laugh. Her laughter was hypnotic.

"I think I might have a spare at home," Marc joked. The two chuckled.

After an awkward silence Marc said, "Seriously, though, Lareina. If you need anything, please don't hesitate to call me."

"I won't, Detective. When I get out of here, I'd really like to do something to thank you for saving me."

"You don't need to thank me. Seeing you here and knowing that you're getting better is all the thanks that I need."

"Detective, you are too kind."

"Please, call me Marc."

"Ok, Marc." Once again, Lareina's smile gleamed.

Marc couldn't help but to smile as well. Lareina's smile had an inebriating effect on him.

"I'm glad to see you're doing so much better," he said. "You were so badly beaten up: it was actually painful to see you in such a condition."

"Yeah, I wasn't the prettiest of sights when you rescued me."

"No, no, Lareina. I didn't mean it that way. It wasn't like that at all.

"It's just - I've been doing this for a long time, Lareina. I've seen some horrible things over the years. But to see an innocent person such as yourself be so badly abused and mistreated just really got to me. Yours was one of my worst cases of human torture."

"That's me: I like to be memorable," she tried to make light of her trauma. "At least I know you won't forget me."

"I could never forget you, Lareina," Marc replied.

"Thank you. I do appreciate your concern and kindness. It's nice to know that you actually cared." She sighed at the thought of all that had transpired. "I'll admit it, though, Marc. There were times I was truly scared. There were times where I really didn't know if I would survive or not. I still don't know how I was able to last as long as I did."

"You're an incredible woman, Lareina. You're very strong, amazingly creative and sharp witted. You're very much a fighter. I don't think you realize just how brave, strong and resilient you truly are. There are very few people who would be able to do all that you did to help lead us to you. You have an incredible, unbreakable spirit. That is how you survived."

Lareina blushed a little. "Thank you."

Marc sighed softly. "Well, I guess I should go, you were trying to rest and I disturbed you."

"No, no. Not at all. You didn't disturb me, Marc.

"It's actually really good to see you again. I'm so thrilled you stopped by. Thank you so much for everything."

"It's good to see you too, Lareina. You're more than welcome. You take care, ok?"

"I will. You too."

"Good night." Marc's voice was so gentle and sweet. It was such a pleasant sound to her ears. She watched him leave her hospital room and fade out into the hallway.

Lareina sighed, and went to sleep with a smile on her face.

Chapter 20

Marc flashed his charming British smile. "You know, I don't normally go out to dinner with my rescues."

"I just wanted some way to thank you, Marc. If it weren't for you, I wouldn't be alive. You are my knight in shining armor.

"I figured dinner was the least I could do to properly thank you," Lareina said.

"Well, I owe you thanks as well. I'll admit that I've never had anyone fight to save me before. Thank you for fighting back."

"That was nothing," Lareina dismissed her actions. "You had finally come to save me; I couldn't allow anything to happen to you. Tony had hurt enough people. I wasn't going to let him hurt anyone any more.

"It was the least I could do considering all the work you did to come rescue me."

They were seated at a quiet table at an elegant restaurant in Santa Monica. It was a quiet, personal, and exquisite setting.

There was something different about Marc. Lareina had truly wanted to thank him, yet there was something inside her that stirred and she was simply thrilled at the opportunity to see him again.

"How are you holding up?" He asked as he gently placed his hand on top of hers.

"I think I'm doing alright. I just finished the antibiotics for the wound on my leg. The doctors said there was some deep muscle damage, but they did say it looks like I'm healing well. The slash on my arm is completely healed. It's left a scar, but it could have been much worse. I still have some minor fractures in my ribs and hands that are healing slowly. The doctors seem so optimistic that I think I'm doing well over all. I go to physical therapy three times a week. And they also tell me I'm making very good progress, so that's good.

"I'm going through trauma counseling as well. I go twice a week to that. They've put me on some medications to help with the panic attacks and nightmares. That helps somewhat.

"I took this semester off so that I could focus on getting better before I go back to that hectic schedule. I will finish school, but I just need some personal time right now."

Lareina paused for a moment; her demeanor and tone brightened. "Would you believe I get calls for my story daily? Newspapers, publishers – I even got a call about a movie deal! I keep telling them to leave me alone, but they are persistent!"

Lareina softly laughed, the lighting in the room caused a beautiful twinkle in her eyes.

"That's Los Angeles for you," Marc smiled.

Lareina smiled back at the handsome man who sat before her. She paused to look down at her plate, thinking back to all the events that led them to meet. She quietly sighed. "In all seriousness, though, Sandy and I are talking about getting a trained guard dog. Just so that we can both feel at ease with everything. Between the media constantly hounding us and knowing that there are people like Tony out there, I think we'd both feel a lot better with a dog."

"That's not a bad idea, Lareina. I can speak to some of the officers in the canine unit, if you like. I can see if we can help you get you trainer or breeder names or something."

"Oh that is so sweet of you, Marc. Thank you. I would really appreciate it." Lareina paused. "I really appreciate everything you've done for me." Her eyes reflected a strong, intense sincerity. They were so alluring – too alluring - for Marc to resist. Marc turned away to hide the fact that he blushed.

"It's alright. It's all part of the job."

"Well, thank you, nonetheless."

Marc looked back up at Lareina. Her hazel eyes drew him in. He was paralyzed by her beauty. "You're more than welcome, Lareina."

The two continued enjoying their dinner, their surroundings, and their company.

When they had finally finished the extravagant meal, the waitress placed the bill in the middle of the table and Marc grabbed it before Lareina.

"No, Marc, wait. I was the one who asked you to dinner. I am supposed to pay."

"I appreciate the gesture, Lareina. I believe that regardless, a gentleman should always pay. It would actually be my pleasure."

Lareina's smile was warm and wide. "Ok, if you insist," she replied.

After paying the bill, Marc had an idea. "Let's take a stroll down to the pier, shall we?"

"I would love to!"

As they left the restaurant, Marc said, "After you."

As he came up from behind her, he lightly placed his hand on the small of her back. She looked behind her and then turned to her right side as he came and walked beside her. She smiled at him, and he at her.

They took a leisurely stroll down to the Santa Monica Pier past all the people, the carnival rides, and the various snack stands. They walked down to the end of the pier and they stood watching the sun slowly make its way down towards the water. The sun was reflected in the infinite Pacific Ocean as a bright orange orb. Seagulls and loons flew overhead and would occasionally dive into the water. Silently, they each took in the peace and tranquility of the scene before them. Marc's hand never left Lareina's back. This was a special moment in paradise they were sharing.

After some time, Marc noticed how low the sun sat in the sky. As much as he wanted to stay there, he still feared for Lareina's safety. He wanted to be sure that she was home before dark.

"We should go," he softly whispered in her ear. "I don't want you getting home too late."

Lareina looked up at the handsome man. As much as she, too, hated the idea of leaving she knew he was right.

As they began to leave the pier, the chilly ocean air began to nip at Lareina. Marc could see she was getting cold. Marc put his arm around her to keep her warm and protected. It was very comforting to her. It felt good - almost natural - to have his arm around her. It was a wonderful feeling that she could easily get used to.

They arrived at her truck too soon. They looked at each other intensely.

"So x equals two, eh? What exactly does that mean?" Marc lightly asked.

"Well, two is a unique number. It's the only even prime number.

"When I was in high school, the first algebraic equation that I did had an answer of x equals two. I was so proud of myself for getting it, and that was when I realized that algebra was my talent and passion. I don't know, that was something that always just stuck with me, I guess.

"It actually kind of applies to the kidnapping, too."

"Really? How is that?"

"Well you see, if you take the values of the coordinates of the cabin and make them into decimal values and add them together you get a total of one hundred fifty six point six. Now, if you add my age to Tony's age, you get seventy. If you take the one fifty six point six and divide it by seventy, you get an answer of two point two. Round it down to two: it's close enough!

"Who says algebra isn't applicable in every day life?" Lareina chuckled.

Marc looked at Lareina. He was impressed by her brilliance, and her candidness in speaking about her trauma.

"Besides, it's better to be two than one." She gently nudged him with a large grin on her face.

"Thank you again," Lareina whispered. She then stood up on her toes and kissed Marc on the cheek.

Marc smiled a wide, bright, elated smile. "You're welcome." He opened the car door for Lareina as she got in. He stood in front of it, so not even the truck's door could be a barrier between him and the Hispanic beauty.

"Ummmm...if it's ok, I'd like to see you again, Marc. If it's not against protocol or anything," Lareina said.

Marc's smile continued to grow. "No, no. It's not against protocol. I would be honored, Lareina."

The two stared at each other, both smiling and flushing with color.

Finally, Marc took and held Lareina's delicate face in both of his large hands, and pulled himself to her and gently kissed her. It was warm, it was passionate, it was tender. This kiss was so different from anything either had ever experienced before. It was so soft, yet so exuberant. It was sweet, and neither wanted it to end. The spark between them was undeniable.

Eventually, their lips slowly parted. Again, they simply smiled at each other.

"Call me when you get home, so I know you're alright," Marc whispered.

"I will," Lareina replied quietly.

Her eyes lit up and flirted with his for endless moments.

"You should probably go, it's getting dark. I don't want you to be in the dark alone," Marc said with genuine concern.

"Thank you. I guess you're right. I should get going."

As Marc gently closed the door to the truck he said, "Don't forget to call me when you get in."

"I won't," Lareina smiled as the door closed.

Through the open truck window, Marc again softly kissed the beautiful woman who sat before him. It was so intense, so beautiful. Lareina hated the idea of leaving this man, and this kiss.

Unwillingly, Marc pulled away. "I'll talk to you in a little while," he said softly.

"Yes, definitely." Lareina replied with a large smile.

Hesitantly, she started the truck. They smiled at each other one last time as Marc stepped back. He watched her slowly pull away.

"I might have rescued her, but she rescued my heart," he thought to himself as he slowly walked back to his car.

Epilogue

Marc and Lareina sat at a table at an exclusive restaurant in Beverly Hills.

"What's the occasion?" Lareina asked.

"Do I have to have an occasion? I can't just take you here because I love you?"

Lareina smiled.

The past two years had flown by. Tony's trial went quickly, but still it had been rather painful and traumatic for Lareina. Both Marc and Lareina were relieved that Tony had received the maximum sentence possible: he wouldn't be up for parole for at least twenty five years. He also suffered severe spinal damage as a result from the rock Lareina threw at him. He would forever be physically disabled thanks to her bravery.

Lareina would be graduating with her doctorate later this year. UCLA offered her a position as a full-time professor immediately following her graduation.

Marc continued to work as a missing persons detective with the LAPD.

After the kidnapping, Lareina wanted her life to be somewhat normal again. She continued to live with Sandy and tried to maintain the life she had before the trauma, though she and Marc had begun dating.

Marc and Lareina shared an incredible chemistry together. Their meeting was truly destiny. Their relationship had blossomed beautifully over the past two years. She still had yet to make love with him, though. She wanted to live her life according to her beliefs, and her trauma from Tony's rape still haunted her. Marc fully understood, and was completely patient with Lareina. He loved their relationship, and refused to ruin it. Lareina was a treasure he was not going to lose.

Lareina's parents and Juanito had been reintroduced to Marc at the trial. Instead of holding the position of the lead investigator of their daughter's kidnapping case, Marc was now her friend, her confidant, and her suitor. They all liked him. The family greatly approved of their relationship.

After placing their orders with the waiter, Marc stared deeply into Lareina's eyes. Lareina lightly blushed.

"Lareina, I have a question for you," Marc spoke gently.

"Ok?" Lareina was puzzled by the rather serious tone in Marc's voice. She had not heard him speak like that in a long while.

"I have already spoken to your family, and they said yes."

"Ok?" Lareina looked at him, perplexed.

"Well, I was wondering," Marc said as he reached into his coat pocket. "If you would marry me."

Marc presented a small black box, inside was an exquisite ring with one large princess cut diamond, surrounded by smaller diamonds.

Lareina gasped at the ring, and the proposal. She looked up at Marc, her eyes were already tearing. "Yes, of course!" Her voice quaked. She ran over to him and the two hugged. The shared a quick, but special kiss before Marc placed the opulent ring on Lareina's delicate little hand.

As she sat back down Marc said, "Lareina, you're the most incredible woman I know. You are the epitome of strength and resiliency. You are so amazingly sharp and intelligent. I love you so much. I'm honored that you will be my wife."

"I love you too, Marc!"

The two could not stop smiling or laughing throughout their entire dinner. This night was a night they both had only dreamed of.

Marc drove them back to his apartment after dinner. He opened the car door for Lareina. As soon as she stepped out, he swept her up and carried her over the threshold of his apartment.

"Wait, silly!" Lareina said as she sat in his broad, muscular arms. "You're not supposed to do that until after we're married!"

"I'll do it then, too." Marc smiled and tenderly kissed Lareina.

Gently he put her down, only to have her embrace him tightly. She felt so safe and so comfortable in his arms.

"I love you, Marcus Raymer," she said looking up and deeply into his chocolate brown eyes.

"I love you too, the soon-to-be-Mrs. Raymer. Actually, that would be Doctor Raymer, now wouldn't it?" His smile was infinite.

Lareina shrieked with giddiness and excitement. "We have to a pick a date!"

Marc paused to think. "Hmmm...how about tomorrow?"

Lareina smiled. "I'd love to, but you know I need to get a drop-dead gorgeous dress!"

"Oh, fine," Marc teased.

Lareina stood up on her toes and kissed Marc. It was a deep, loving, passionate kiss. His lips were soft and warm. He wrapped his large arms around her tiny body. She held his face in both of her soft hands. They continued in this passionate kiss that became sensual. Lareina had never felt like this before. The tingle that she experienced throughout her entire body was exhilarating.

She began to run her hands over his muscular chest. Touching him felt incredible to Lareina. She craved more – she wanted to feel his warm skin against her own. For the first time, her body yearned for his. She was ready to fully give herself to him completely: mind, soul, and now her body.

Gently, she unbuttoned each of the tiny buttons on his dress shirt. It eventually drifted to the ground. Lareina pressed herself into his warm chest even more. His bare skin felt good against her. She continued to trace his muscles lightly with her fingers over his bare skin; she didn't want this feeling, or this moment to end. Slowly, as she still sensuously kissed Marc, she allowed her hands to make their way down to the rim of his pants.

Marc gently pulled away. "Wait. Lareina, are you sure? I don't want to hurt you."

"Yes, Marc. I'm sure. You're going to be my husband soon. I love you and trust you with all my heart and soul. I know you won't hurt me."

Marc looked into her glistening hazel eyes. "Are you sure?" He repeated himself.

"Yes."

Marc gently took Lareina by the hand and led her to his bedroom. He sat on the bed and pulled her into him. They resumed their amazing kiss.

Lareina's hands gently rested on Marcs large shoulders. Marc placed his hands on her hips. Then his large hands began to move and explore all of Lareina's small, curvaceous body. Lareina began to unbutton her blouse while Marc still caressed her through her clothes.

Once her blouse and bra reached the floor, Marc stopped again and looked up at Lareina. There was an incredible vulnerability to her beautiful but scarred and naked body. Marc did not want to take advantage of her; she appeared seemingly helpless. He greatly feared hurting her. Lareina could see the concern in his deep brown eyes. She smiled down at him, and simply nodded.

Marc's large, warm hands slowly and carefully felt every inch of Lareina's soft, supple skin. Eventually, his hands were back on her hips. He cautiously moved them forward and gently unbuttoned and unzipped her pants; they pooled around her tiny ankles.

Lareina's little hands went to Marc's large belt. With a bit of difficulty, Lareina managed to take off his belt, and then undo his pants.

The couple stayed in their open, vulnerable, naked state sharing a loving kiss and emotions that neither of them had experienced before. Slowly, Marc stood up, picked up Lareina and gently placed her on his bed. Though she was exposed and vulnerable, she felt safe and protected with Marc.

He gently placed himself on top of her, and slowly slid himself inside her beautiful body. Lareina's body shuddered with excitement.

They made love for hours, sharing passion, ecstasy, and endless love.

Afterwards, Lareina curled up and nestled herself into the warmth and safety of Marc's muscular arm. He smiled as he was feeling her wonderful, warm body against his. She softly lay her head on his chest. She could hear his heart beat. It was the greatest sound she had ever heard.

"I love you Marc," she whispered as she dozed off into a peaceful sleep, resting in the arms of her rescuer, fiancé, and lover.

More Great Books by Lauren Shiro

Imperfect

Carol Mathers, in her mid-thirties, a highly sought-after IT guru in St. Louis. She has built a great life for herself with her partner, Alexandria, even though the two face prejudice as lesbians, and as an interracial couple -fighting tragedy and sometimes, triumphing amidst the chaos...

Impeccable

Carol – abandoned - waiting... for what, she couldn't know. She couldn't see that there was more life waiting for her. Carol is forced to face the demons of her past as well as begin to face life without Alex. Struggling to make sense of it all, Carol experiences her new life and all of the highs and lows that come with that life.

Loving Her, the series

Loving Her is a collection of short stories celebrating love and life between women; each story tells a story, and together, they create a depth and understanding of women's love for each other and for life. Loving Her shares the stories of remarkable and ordinary women- women learning to love and women making a difference, all while managing the world around them...as lovers do.

Amnesie, a short story

What happens to love when life changes? Two women in love, one debilitating change...

Trajectory, a short story

Joe Davis has spent the last four years of his life behind a scope as a sniper for the Detroit PD's SWAT Team. A fateful call sends Joe and his team deep into the Detroit Ghetto; and reminds him that there is more to life than what's on the other end of his gun.

Lauren Shiro was published nationally for the first time at age fourteen. Since then, her work has been published in newspapers, magazines, literary journals, and even textbooks.

In 2006, she began writing fiction and she hasn't stopped yet. From her set of intertwined short stories in Loving Her, to the powerhouse duo of Imperfect and Impeccable, Lauren has written stories that are sure to touch your heart. Lauren continues to write stories of love without boundaries.

When she's not writing, Lauren works as a licensed veterinary technician. In her spare time, she enjoys everything from wood working to roller derby. She resides in Rochester, New York with her wife and their menagerie of furry and feathered friends.

Love without Boundaries

In celebration of her one year wedding anniversary and recent political changes that legalize her marriage, author Lauren E. Harvey (L. E. Harvey) and Vanilla Heart Publishing are excited to announce the re-releases of her books and a brand new series of Loving Her singles with her (legal) married name, Lauren Shiro.